# Skye

## A Heart in the Heather

CeCe deLuc

# DEDICATION

I got my love of writing from my Dad, and I'm grateful for it every day. He encouraged me from my earliest attempt when I was 8. I am sure he knew then that I never would have another opportunity to use my most original line – *"The queen was so mad you could fry an egg on her!"* so Dad published it in a column he wrote for a local newspaper. I'm proud he found me quotable then, and I hope he's looking down proudly on some of my more recent writing.

It's a valuable skill to have inherited, and I treasure it.

And, in answer to that whisper of "write, Meg, write," I hear in my ears every so often.

"Yes, Dad. I'm writing."

# ACKNOWLEDGMENTS

While this book imagines a character dealing with post-traumatic stress resulting from the Boston Marathon bombing, it recognizes a changing world and embraces love as a tool for healing. While 911 brought a new definition to terrorism coming home to America, for me, the Boston Marathon bombing brought it even closer. In a world of wars, violent protests, and epic hate being practiced on one another, I hope this book brings you back to love for a while.

# CHAPTER 1

The blood was everywhere, soaking the victim's garments and Lily's scrubs, leading from the ambulance to the bed on which he now lay bleeding out. Bits of shrapnel clung to pieces of skin, and he was silent -- but the room was loud. Half a dozen voices were shouting a hundred commands. All of them accomplished with competency and military precision.

Surgeons and ER docs; nurses and orderlies – all joining together to save this one.

And yet, in the next room was another with similar grievous injuries; and in the next room, another; and so on.

Lily knew how this would end – the victim in front of her would die soon – the blood he needed to survive came out as soon as it went in. No transfusion would hold. He was just too severely damaged. His legs – both of them, were missing – almost certainly still out on Boylston Street. If they had been salvageable, the EMTs would have brought them to the hospital. Besides the missing legs, his abdomen was ripped apart. His organs were intact, but his belly needed a thousand stitches.

Maybe two thousand.

Lily had steeled herself when she took this job to remain compassionate but emotionless. ER work was often traumatic, and she needed to cope with the day-to-day to avoid burnout. Nevertheless, there would always be days that tested her faith in humanity and God. Today was one.

"Ahhhhhhhhhhhhh!"

Lily reached out and squeezed his hand.

Sometimes a reassuring touch was all that was needed to ease someone out of this world. But she was surprised when he squeezed back – firmly.

"I'm gonna make it, you know. You're looking at me as if I won't see the end of the hour or the end of the day – but I will. I'm stronger than they are. I'll live." And Lily believed him.

"Andrew, I know you're strong, but you

have a fight ahead of you," Lily said with a catch in her voice.

"Ah, but don't you know, my name means 'warrior'. I was born to fight this. And when I'm done, and I'm back up and walking again, I will be after finding the men who did this to me."

"I believe you will."

Lily remembered his words as she slipped into bed 15 hours later. There was tired, and there was exhausted. But this feeling of being out of control and in a new and ugly world persisted, despite remembering Andrew Donnelly. He had survived and would be spending many months in hospital, at rehab, and at home. But he would live. That was a win.

As she lay, tossing and turning, she thought about the many others who wouldn't survive -- children, parents, lovers -- a 20-year-old girl who'd bled out because she kept pressure on her boyfriend's neck wound, ignoring her own injuries – a missing leg and an arm in tatters.

Her heroic attempts were in vain.

The boyfriend she'd met in Lit class at the beginning of Winter Term died also.

In all, 5 people had died -- many of them

at the hospital where Lily worked. There were too many injured to count, being treated at hospitals across the city. Lily had stopped in the chapel at the hospital and offered a long prayer for the seen and unseen victims of the day. She prayed for them to be saved, silently acknowledging to herself, many wouldn't.

But Andrew's determination stood out for her, and she added a plea for him.

None of these thoughts helped her sleep—the mental fatigue keeping her mind spinning long after her body surrendered.

Finally, 2 hours later, Lily knew what she had to do.

She reached over to her cell phone and dialed a number.

"Ah. I knew I'd be hearing from you, my love." The voice on the other end answered.

"Oh, Fife! It was terrible."

# CHAPTER 2

**"** Ok, Andrew – I know you'd rather play Zelda than get up, but you promised me – today we are going on a walk." Lily threw off the blankets covering Andrew's legs – or, to be more specific – stumps.

"Nurse Griffin - Lily, we walked the other day. Don't feel like it today."

"Well, it's too bad, Andrew. Yesterday was my day off, or you'd have walked then, also. You made me a promise three months ago that you'd survive, and you will, but if you're just going to lie in bed and play video games, what's the point? I quit my job at the hospital because I believed in your promise. I followed you to this rehab center - I've done my part. Your turn!" Lily, all the while tossing clothes at him and organizing his prostheses.

Andrew knew that he owed his life to Lily

– and he was eternally grateful, but the funk he was in now seemed impenetrable. The phantom pain from the limbs he lost kept him up at night, giving him hours to think about his bleak future. Trained as a cop before being sidelined by two terrorists, he couldn't see forward to his future.

Andrew had spent a considerable part of the time since his injury talking with therapists – for his physical and emotional health, and he felt at a standstill. What was next for a cop with no legs who wanted justice? Today, if he weren't walking on his own two feet – and he wasn't, he would play Zelda. Strategize his life.

Lily knew that Andrew was way ahead of the curve in his recovery, but it truly upset her to see him skip a chance to walk – especially with her going away for a month.

"Andrew – I know you're tired of how hard everything is but look at what you've accomplished! You are not that guy I thought would die right in front of me three months ago. YOU survived. Don't stop now! I'm going away for a while, and I want to know that you will work toward your goal while I'm gone. That you'll improve." Lily said in as even a voice as she was able. He'd become so important to her.

"Listen, Lily – go. Just go. I don't want to

work out today, and I might not tomorrow. I make no promises for when you're away. But you go – you take a break from this awfulness. You're looking sickly." Andrew hadn't meant to sound cruel. But he had. He knew how hard Lily had worked to help him survive and recover, and it had played out on her. She was pale and thin, drawn. The twinkle he'd imagined in her eyes gone.

He had a plan for while she was away, and he needed to rest up for that.

Sensing something was up, Lily said, "Fine – see you in a month!" and closed the door. She had to force herself away from him because she felt such pity for him – and now because he was letting her down – anger.

This vacation for her was essential. She needed to recharge. Her faith in humanity had suffered a blow that day in April. But her faith in the survival instinct had come through. So, for now, Andrew was right – she needed to take herself out of the situation and heal herself.

Fife would help her do that.

Lily wasn't sure she could cope with life right now without spending some time with Fife. He grounded her. There was a calmness about him and an air of protection and confidence. And she knew he'd understand better than anyone else in her life what those days in Boston had been like – he'd been in a war also.

Lily liked her job – always had. She'd rotated out of the pediatric ward to the ER two years earlier. Lily wanted to challenge herself. After the first week in the ER, Lily realized she'd made the right choice. She was embarrassed to say she enjoyed the adrenaline rush she experienced when a new patient came in, whether a sprained ankle or a heart attack. She enjoyed the challenge of diagnosing and fixing whatever she was presented with.

Her work as a nurse had always brought her satisfaction, but now it didn't. She wanted to heal people, but she'd let herself get so depressed and depleted that she couldn't help Andrew properly. So, she would heal.

# CHAPTER 3

A s she gazed out the airplane window at sunrise over the Atlantic, she began to feel hopeful. This trip would be a new beginning for her. And then, when she went home, she would be able to help Andrew.

The view of Portree Harbor and its rainbow of houses on Skye never failed to take Lily's breath away. She loved this place above all the others she'd visited. Not only because it was home to Fife, and that was special, but it was where she had gone to absorb some of the harder moments of her life. And so, it was notable that she was here now, for something had changed. Not only had Fife asked her to come, and she was glad she was able – but it coincided with a time in her life that had tried her body and soul.

As she exited the hire car at the estate agent's address, she felt a thrill. She was staying for a while – a month for now, and time would tell if that was enough.

As promised, Fife was there to meet her.

In the past 15 years, there hadn't been a visit he'd missed. He was a beloved friend, romantic interest, and a familiar face she couldn't imagine Skye without.

"Ach, my Lily – one foot from the car, and your cheeks are already roses, and there is a peace in the set of your shoulders. I know you only feel here. "Welcome!"

Lily observed the tall, handsome redhead as he bounded over to her (he'd thickened a bit over the past fifteen years – but then again, who hadn't), grabbed her in what could only be described as a bear hug, and lifted her off the ground!

"Fife! Put me down! – People will talk!" Lily protested

"I hope people will talk – from their mouths to God's ears -- they usually start after you've left, and it leaves me lonely. Let them talk now, and I will feel complete! You can go in and see Brodie Meath about a place to stay, but I've already chosen.

"What do you mean, YOU'VE chosen?" Despite her affection for this man, Lily couldn't help but get her back up.

She had been in charge of her life for some years and being told where she would live left her with mixed emotions.

Now, considering there'd been much strife in her recent life, she was willing to go along.

"So, what do you have in mind – and what will it cost me?" Lily did her best to keep a smile in her voice.

"The only cost to you will be a few home-cooked meals. Brodie can come too – maybe once. That'll compensate.

"Ok, show me, but let me just thank Brodie first." A little thrill ran through Lily because she knew he wanted her to stay with him – something she knew would change their relationship forever. Six months ago, she'd have objected. But so much had changed.

Lily had met Fife on her first trip to Scotland. At the time, she was hiking in Highlands and twisted her ankle. Fife happened upon her as she tried to fashion a crutch from a large branch. He'd helped her back to her car and kept up a stream of chatter with her the whole time.

By the time she was carefully seated in her car, Fife was her best friend; she knew his whole story – where he'd gone in the service and the fact that he had medical training. Lily, herself a nurse, had held several different positions over the years in numerous departments – at the time in the ICU – Intensive Care Unit. This common thread bound them together. Although now Fife had a construction company and was 'building an empire' – his words.

Her trip at that time was only ten days, but most of them spent with Fife and Annis, Fife's mother. They immersed her in the life of their village so that by the time she left, she had a crowd to see her off. Each year she came back, and her circle grew. These were her people now, and she knew she was theirs.

Snapping back to attention, "I'll just pop into Brodie's."

Fife watched her go and thought she looked healthy but tired. At 5' 4", she wasn't a tall woman, and she looked a bit like the French character Madeline from the picture books his niece brought with her when his brother visited from America.

After a brief, apologetic chat with Old Brodie – the kindest man in Portree, Lily got into Fife's little green car, and they sped through the harbor and up the hill.

There, on a promontory, Lily knew was Fife's family home. His mother was all that was left now – his brother Donal had emigrated to America 20 years ago, and as a matter of fact – Lily hadn't ever met him. Annis, Fife's mother, was a dear friend and advisor to Lily now. Annis didn't have email, but she and Lily exchanged letters throughout the year. Annis could be counted on to appeal to Lily at least once or twice a year to come and marry Fife.

She realized that they were driving past Fife's cottage now with no sign of him slowing down. Then she realized where he was stopping, in front of the old henhouse, which now looked gloriously different, triple the size, and cleaned up– a stone patio added out front, fitted with outside furniture – a love seat and chairs, surrounding a fire pit and overlooking the harbor. There was a fresh whitewash on the stucco, and the windows were open; crisp white muslin curtains blowing in and out.

"Here? Fife! It's lovely – when did you redo it? Last year it was a run-down old henhouse with a million-dollar view!" Lily was stunned.

Arguably, this was the best view, the best location in the Scottish Isles, and it was Fife's.

"I did a bit of work on it after you left last year after you said that it was the best place on the island, and you couldn't believe the hens had it!" Come inside – I made sure it was comfortable, and I brought in a bit of supplies.

Inside was a dream! Everything was new but looked like it had been made for it – and it was considerably bigger looking inside rather than out.

It wound like a snake with sudden annexes, tiny little rooms with no purpose but charm. And Lily realized it was more like five times the size of the old hen house. For example, there was a room probably no bigger than 5 feet square, the only purpose of which was to display vintage dishes and vases. It opened into another room with a window, 4 or 5 feet wide and 2 feet tall – cranked open to the breeze. A desk sat in front of it – an easy chair covered in white poplin in a corner with a pale pink overstuffed chenille pillow propped in it. A round shaggy white rug in the middle of the room begged for toes to be squished into it. The muslin curtains she'd noted outside graced this window, and a vase of lavender sat on the right corner of the desk. As the wind blew gently, the fresh smell of lavender perfumed the room.

To the right of that room was the kitchen – a deep blue Aga cooker being the primary color in the room. The floor was slate with occasional white rugs splashed around. A white porcelain farmers' sink sat beneath three pairs of double-hung windows, white granite countertops, and glass-fronted white cupboards above.

Below were white cabinets where on inspection, Lily found all manner of pots and pans. A lavender-blue painted cupboard against the right wall was inscribed 'Pantry' and indeed contained any supply she'd ever need. A newish-looking refrigerator in white was to the left of the Aga. The left-hand wall had another large window, similar to the one in the study and a companion chair sat beside it.

The middle of the kitchen contained a refectory table in dark wood and held nothing but a vase of wildflowers and a statue of a hen. Perfect.

"Fife, this is beautiful. It must have cost you thousands...."

"Wait, you haven't seen the rest." Lily could hear the pride in Fife's voice, and she knew how much this meant to him.

Beside the pantry cupboard was another doorway leading to a hallway lined with French windows on both sides – the bay of Portree to the left and a courtyard to the right. At the end of the corridor was an opening into a bedroom – not huge but luxurious – with pale floral wallpaper, a fluffy white rug, an iron bed, and windows on three sides! The remaining wall that held the doorway had a fireplace and a cozy sitting area. Finally, the left side had a door to what Lily expected was the bathroom – and it was. A claw-footed bath sat beneath the ubiquitous windows, the floor alternating purple and white squares. Off that, in another random jog, was a laundry room fitted with new equipment and painted a fresh light green, holding a wall of closets.

Lily was astonished at the amount of work and money that had gone into designing and completing this charming home.

"I've put heat under the floor – thought it was a nice luxury on this chilly coast."

"I love it – but is there a lounge – a living room? Lily asked.

"Yes – the best for last. Follow me."

And she did -- back through the kitchen and the study into the little room with the china, and out the other side of it – to a sunken living room furnished in natural tones to match the stone fireplace that looked large enough to stand in – and encircled by deep leather couches and chaises with white throws that resembled meringues.

"This is the winter lounge. You also could have accessed it from the bedroom. Follow me to the garden lounge." Fife added.

Lily followed Fife – she had no choice, as he held her hand and gave her a tug. He opened a double set of French doors to a small bright hallway with a powder room to the right, furnished in a sunny yellow, and through another set of French Doors to the most beautiful room, Lily had ever seen.

The Garden Lounge was bliss – one entire wall was made up of French doors, and the seagrass-green rug balanced the white in the room – white over-stuffed couches with bright blues and greens and violets for pillows. There was a fireplace here too, but it was surrounded by whitewashed pine and was furnished with a multitude of candles. The drapes on the walls were a whiff of pale lilac and reminded her of the clouds over the loch during a summer storm.

Stretched out on the end of the white chaise was a tiny golden kitten with a lavender collar.

"Lily – this is Ailie – she is yours if you'll stay. As am I."

Fife's voice became gruff, and Lily felt the pressure on her hand increase as he squeezed it,

"Fife, this is wonderful, but I've only just got here, and you know what I've been up against recently. Can we delay this talk for a bit so I can get my head back in the heather?"

He smiled because he knew what she meant. Getting her head in the heather was surrendering her stress to the beauty of this spot, letting go of the worry and reveling in the wonder of Skye.

"My darlin', I know where to find you, and you can't leave without seeing me, so I know I'll have an answer."

"Ok then – let me take a soak in that luxurious bathtub. I'll rustle some dinner up for us, and we can talk. Come back in a couple of hours."

Fife liked the fact that she was looking forward to a tub – he knew she needed pampering, and he was willing to provide it. And he knew he'd made her happy. So, with a snappy salute – "Aye, aye, Madam – I'll bring some wine. See you at seven," he took his leave.

Thirty minutes later, Lily was up to her neck in a bubble bath. She hadn't had one since she was ten, but this tub just cried out for it.

The walls of this little jewel of a bathroom were lined with glass jars full of bath salts and special soaps.

There were line drawings of the moors on the walls, fluffy towels, and deep pile rugs spread over the floor.

Ailie, the kitten, was rolling around the floor, playing with a purple ribbon that had fallen out of the drawer where Lily had found a face cloth.

# CHAPTER 4

Lily leaned her head against the bath pillow Fife had thoughtfully included and closed her eyes. Now she could relax and think about what had brought her here without panic and guilt. She knew she'd done what she should and would do it again. But in the dark of night in her bed, she often wondered why it fell to her team to save the savage. And why they couldn't.

The horror of that day and that week never left her. She could see the carnage as it came in the door, and as a nurse, she had to remove her emotions from the thing. She needed to perform and not cry.

In addition to Andrew, it was the Cullen Brothers that got to her. They were 25 and 30 years old and should have been full of bravado. Instead, they were weak and vulnerable. Their whole lives were changed in the time it took to put down a backpack. The older one was in agonizing pain from terrible injuries he'd suffered but wouldn't leave the ER for surgery until he knew his younger brother would survive. The younger Cullen, suffering from similar monumental injuries, was unconscious until after his sibling had been rolled away. When he woke, it was to darkness – the explosion had robbed him of his left eye and his sight. His panic was hard to quell, and he only calmed when his mother came to sit beside him.

She held his hand and whispered to him, but he couldn't see the tears that ran in rivers down her face and the sad slope of her shoulders. He couldn't see her recoil in horror at the condition he was in and the anticipation of what lay ahead for him.

He went to surgery soon after that, but for Lily, the nightmare continued as patient after patient came in.

She spent four solid hours picking shrapnel out of the wounds on a young girl's legs and torso. Finally, Lily knew little Natalie would be ok when she said, "Do you have a lot of bandages? 'Cuz we're going to need a lot."

Lily smiled and produced a box, and Natalie was satisfied. Natalie wasn't critically injured but in shock and would need more than bandages to heal her.

At the end of that terrible shift, Lily didn't have the strength to go home, but she needed to talk to someone. She had spent some time decompressing with her co-workers and had even helped to calm one of the younger nurses who was near hysterical after working with their ER chief to put a patient back together. Unfortunately, the woman's injuries were savage. Like several others, her stomach and legs torn open.

Sally, the young nurse, had promised Enid that she'd survive – the woman couldn't have been more than 30 years old. But she'd lost too much blood before the ambulance had brought her in and ultimately couldn't be saved. With her limited experience, Sally had never seen such butchery in person, and her reaction, while not the norm in the ER, was not the only one that day. Too much savagery to so many people. There was anger among the staff, tears were shed, and prayers were offered. Every reaction a valid one - healers need healing too. The nurses and docs knew there was an end to their day, but the battle had ended permanently or was only just beginning for some that they treated.

And it was personal to all who'd tried to help.

A call to her parents made her feel better, and they were relieved she was all right, but that wasn't all she needed. Lily needed someone to tell her they had been through something similar, and they'd survived. And so, she called Fife.

Fife understood because he'd been in Iraq and Afghanistan, had seen horrific wounds, and had seen survival. He'd been a medic out of Scotland, and he knew that the tragedy that came to Boston that day was also from a war.

Fife's words had the intended result on Lily, and he left her feeling better. The following days were hard, but Lily had a grip on it now, until that Friday night. Then, she knew when the ER began to fill up with 1st responders that something else had happened.

By the time the evening was over, Lily was covered in the blood of the Architect of all that earlier chaos.

This time, despite the extraordinary means available to them, they couldn't save him. He died without explanation and without paying for the carnage he had caused. There wasn't survival, and good didn't prevail. Instead, there was a hole where redemption should have been. As the primary nurse that night, Lily felt she hadn't done enough to ensure that Andrew, the Cullen Brothers, and the others had a chance at justice.

Never a believer or supporter of the death

penalty, she was forced to adapt to what had happened. While her soul demanded that he live for justice to be served, she had to acknowledge that she had no control over the outcome.

This time Fife had been unable to give the words that consoled her. She knew that she wasn't alone in trying to save the terrorist. But it felt that way.

Fife knew she was in a dark place.

That was three months ago, and he'd called her a few times each week to encourage her to come. But she had Andrew to get well. Lily had taken her commitment to Andrew to heart and had followed him to the rehab hospital he'd gone to after discharge. She felt wholly responsible for Andrew's recovery. Fife understood a mission like that.

In the end, she agreed to go to Skye because she'd stopped sleeping, and the rehab hospital had prevailed on her to rest. Being in this magical place only a few hours had softened the edges of her grief and had reminded her that life was for the living.

On that happy thought, she realized the tub water had grown cold, and she had dinner to prepare.

# CHAPTER 5

An hour later, the chicken was bubbling away in the Aga, and two seats were set at the refectory table. Fife's taste was impeccable and a perfect match for Lily's. She set the table with homey white placemats, the fine silver she found in the drawers, and a pretty set of ivory pottery. Wine glasses were situated at each place.

A knock on the door announced Fife's arrival, and she excitedly rushed to answer. He came in smelling of the sea and toothpaste. The wind had spun color into his handsome face, and his red hair had a curl in the middle. He had dressed casually in a blue sweater and jeans. He was stunning, and Lily was glad she'd dressed similarly. Her style relied heavily on the classics, and tonight her black Capri's and tight black top, and ballet shoes made her the picture of youth, confidence, and happiness.

They kissed when he came in, and Fife told her he had high hopes for this meal. "I've bought you all my favorites – let's see what you've done with them."

"Mmmm, Chicken and Rice – oh and little, tiny peas! Please tell me there is Chocolate Cake for dessert – I think I smell Chocolate. "

"Yes – that baked while I was in your most perfect bathtub," Lily answered.

"Well, with all this effort, I will have to reward you with a fire outside in the fire pit. Then, we'll look over the bay and plan our future." Lily caught his 2nd reference to their future, and she felt her heart begin to beat faster.

For now, she busied herself with getting dinner on the table, putting up coffee to brew while they ate, and fending off Fife's occasional kisses.

She was pleased that he was happy to see her, and she felt the same way, but she'd gotten used to their familiar pattern, and she worried that change would ruin things.

Dinner was delicious and satisfying, and the two of them stayed away from serious topics. Later, after the dinner was cleaned up, she took two mugs of coffee and two slices of Chocolate Cake out to the fire pit where Fife sat on the loveseat.

They enjoyed their dessert, and when the plates were put away, Lily sat next to him, nestled under his arm.

"Darlin,' how are you feeling about things now? I know that these past few months for you have been horrible – do you feel yourself coming out of it now?"

"Fife, I never could have imagined that I would find myself in the midst of such a horrifying chain of events. It frightens me that no matter where I go, I can encounter the same evil. How do you protect yourself? Your family? Where is safety? I'm an independent person, and I have strong faith, but seeing what I have is a sea change I wasn't ready for." Nevertheless, Lily was as honest as she could be with Fife because she knew he understood.

"I know what you mean, my love. My stint in the service opened my eyes, and the only thing I came away with was resolve. I resolve that I will be happy for the rest of the days that are given to me. I will live my best life possible, and I will hope I don't miss any opportunities. That is what I have been given. Optimism and survival, along with forgiveness and curiosity about what else will come. Now is the only time we'll go around together, Lily. In the next life, I could be an ant, and you could be a lioness. Chances are we'll never meet. This time we have is a gift. Let's open it together. Marry me."

Lily looked at Fife and realized that she had been thinking the same way. It was her way of letting go of the horror. To dwell on what was good in her life and strive for a better one. This was meant to be.

"Yes. But..."

"No buts, my love!" Fife directed hastily – unwilling to lose out on her Yes.

"You're marrying me. For sure, this summer! We'll have the fall on the loch and the winter in this cozy home – "

"Fife - I'm not ready to give up my life at home and come here. I need time. I need to get Andrew walking for real and in a job where he's challenged and not thinking about his changed circumstances. I need to see that through to the end!" Lily's voice raised an octave or two. "Listen, I'm just here under 4 hours, and you already are talking to me about changing my life. Doesn't a girl get a little time?" Lily said, now under control.

"Of course, she does – and I don't deny that. I'm just saying that, from my perspective, I'd feel better if OUR life took precedence over Andrew's." Fife instantly regretted his words. He had lingering jealousy over Lily's devotion to Andrew and, ironically, felt great pride in how hard Lily had been working to heal him. So, he was torn, but today the green-eyed monster won.

"Ach, I'm sorry, my love – I should never have said that – You know me, I'm a healer too – not a fighter. Please forget what you heard. But remember this. I love you – have for 15 years and will for 50 more. I'd like our life to start today, but I understand that you aren't ready. I'll wait for you – I think I've proven that – but hurry up!"

"Listen, Fife, I understand where that remark came from, but my feelings are a bit raw right now. Let's forget it. I'll sleep in what I'm sure is a profoundly cozy bed. Wake up and have a long, slow walk in the heather, and I'll be fine. For now, let's say our goodnights. And before I forget. Thank you for making me this house. I love it – and I love you!"

With that, Lily leaned in and kissed Fife gently on the lips and walked back into the hen house.

# CHAPTER 6

The heather did its' work, and by the time Fife had returned for lunch the next day, Lily's equilibrium had returned.

She didn't tell Fife, but she'd called Andrew back at the hospital first thing that morning, and though it was later in the day, she had reached Andrew after his physiotherapy. Andrew was cool with her, but he swore he was coming along fine and that she shouldn't rush back for him. But Lily felt he was harsher than she deserved.

"Listen, Lily, I do appreciate what you've done for me, but I am a man who needs to be in control of his life. I cannot wait for you to spoon-feed me exercises as you see fit. The guy covering for you is tougher with me –I need that. And you remind me of that day far more than my injuries do. Your sad, doe eyes and constant compassionate acceptance are not suited to rehab recovery. You belong in a critical care environment – not in a rehab unit. I can tell you know that – that you know, you need quick results. I will not be quick in my recovery."

"Andrew, I know all of that, but I felt a connection to you and a responsibility to see you recover. You promised ME you would. And if you can wait for me to come back, I will do what I need to get you there."

Andrew was non-committal, and Lily knew he was right about her. A part of her wanted to stay here with Fife – away from danger and drama and damage. She thought about it throughout her relaxing afternoon in the heather and knew that she wasn't ready to go back and face it. She hoped that Andrew would do well without her for now.

Fife was happy to see Lily seeming more resolved to stay awhile – less conflicted. Fife was glad to see it but decided to give her some space for the next few days.

"So, my darling, I know that you've only just gotten here, but I've got to go to the mainland for a few days. I have a big job at a shopping mall there – and they don't perform unless the big man stops in occasionally to rattle the drum. I know you want to rest, so this is probably well-timed. Don't miss me too much." Fife was trying very hard not to let on how much he'd miss her. But he knew this was the right approach.

"Well, I'm disappointed, but I'll visit Annis, have that lovely dinner with Brodie, and will read and relax. Just what I need. Don't be too tough on your team."

"They love me – don't you worry." With that, Fife kissed Lily lingeringly and took his leave. Hoping she'd beg him to stay.

"As do I, Fife – know that. I need to figure out the timing on a few things." Lily explained – concerned that her turning down Fife had already encouraged him toward greener pastures.

"I know that my love but imagine how I feel – you're putting me off for Andrew." With that lingering in the air, Fife left.

Lily was left with her mouth agape. Unable to explain her responsibility to Andrew. Unsure why she'd need to. And finally, unable to ignore her unexpected relief to be staying.

The same thing was on her mind as she got into bed that night, the kitten, Ailie, spooning into Lily's belly. Lily had always felt as if she and Fife were soul mates – that they knew and understood each other on an intimate level. How could the Lily he loved abandon someone who needed her if that were true? Whether it was Andrew or anyone else, it was a dominant personality trait of Lily's – to give care and to never give up! It hurt her and worried her that Fife would expect any less of her. Or that she would demand less of herself. There was a note under the front door when she woke up the following day.

"*My love,*

*Whoops! I did it again! I'm so sorry. I know you need time to get Andrew well, and, honestly, you wouldn't be my Lily if you didn't. So, instead of complaining about why you need more time and giving the green-eyed monster more play, I will spend my energies praying for his swift recovery. At the end of the day, you should be true to yourself first. I love you.*"

*Fife*

Lily felt herself smile from ear to ear - the first genuine one in months!

# CHAPTER 7

L ater that day, after a lengthy chat with Annis and some retail therapy in town, Lily took herself back into the heather. The air was pure up here – there was no pretense and nothing she couldn't trust. Time would tell if she ever felt that way about her hometown again. Lily was having trouble with the prospect of going back. She was strong, she knew, and dedicated to healing Andrew – that was a promise and a commitment. But, at any time, horror could come through the door, just like it had that day in April. She'd tried to block it out, but she'd had trouble sleeping back in Boston, and she feared it had followed her to Skye.

"Come on, Lily – you know that you're not a coward." She told herself. But she'd spent all her energy healing others and had none left for herself. As a nurse, she knew enough to know she likely had post-traumatic stress disorder, but she'd kept it at bay for months now. The rehab hospital had known. But Lily hadn't. Not until she was out here in the air – alone with her thoughts. She knew she had to work through it and knew she couldn't commit to Fife until she did.

She tripped over a small purple rock on her way down the heather. It had blended into the heather almost, but it caused her to stumble a step. It was like a reality slap almost. She was elsewhere right up until that moment when the rock encountered her shoe. It was no more than 3 inches around and flat on one side. She lifted it and found that it was heavy. Her fingers traced the fine lines of the rock, and she realized that it was shaped a bit like a heart, yet there was a piece missing in the middle – an indentation of sorts.

The indentation, which she expected had been worn smooth by time and weather, was rough to the touch. As if it had been broken out – perfectly square. It was a perfect illustration of her life right now – her heart was not broken, but there was a piece missing. Lily acknowledged that she needed to find that piece to move on. Lily pocketed the rock. A talisman for her recovery.

# CHAPTER 8

An hour later, seated in her favorite spot – the writing desk in her little room – she placed the heart rock on a dish she kept there and opened an email that had come while she was out.

*Dear Lily –*

*I wouldn't have survived without you – that's for sure. But I need to take on this beast that is my life now. I am going to live and thrive, but I need to take it from here.*

*Andrew*

There it was – finally. She called her immediate superior back at the hospital in Boston and learned that Andrew had discharged himself. He had checked into a private rehab facility and was under the care of the staff there.

Lily spent the next couple of hours trying

the various private rehab facilities she was familiar with, trying to track down Andrew. Naturally, none of them would confirm that Andrew was a patient – she wasn't surprised – but she felt she had to try. Andrew was her project. She had dedicated herself to his healing. Now – what did this mean to her? *Was she not good enough for him? Had she let him down?* She felt more inadequate than she'd ever felt in her life.

A thought came to her – perhaps Andrew's parents could shed some light on Andrew's status.

Going through her contacts on her phone, she came across a number for them. But they were no help at all –According to Nancy, his mother, he had found a rehab run by a military vet that would take him. She said that Andrew felt that this was his best way to recovery. He wanted hard work to blot out the pain and distract himself from his black view of his future.

Nancy confirmed that Lily hadn't done anything wrong, and Andrew had been grateful for her, but, in the end, he wanted a punishing rehab. Something that would get faster results.

Lily thanked Nancy for her help, but after hanging up the phone, she began to worry about what shortcuts the rehab would take. *Would they work on his mental wounds as well? Would this punishing rehab cause Andrew to have more anger and unrealistic goals?* Lily knew that Andrew was an adult and had put himself in a situation he felt he could control, but she was frustrated that he had essentially fired her despite her investment in his recovery.

Her first inclination was to catch the first ferry to the mainland and get a plane home.

*Would Andrew see me? She* wondered *if I were even able to find out where he went?* But ultimately, she knew that Andrew wanted to move on without her. He'd made as much clear the other day on the phone. It was a harsh reality -- Lily seemed to have become superfluous, which hurt a bit.

Lily went outside and sat on the patio, deep in thought. Her healing, she knew, was directly tied to Andrew's. Even though Andrew's injuries were physical, Lily acknowledged that hers were entirely psychological. She had lost her sense of self that day that the bomber died in her hands. While Lily was against the death penalty and always had been, and she'd tried to save the savage, her soul was pleased he had died. She struggled when she lay down at night – How could Lily be okay with a person in her care dying - how could she call herself a healer?

And what kind of healer is fired by a patient she'd devoted herself to?

She knew that these moral imperatives weighed on many of her colleagues, and more than one of them had sought out therapy, but she couldn't see herself talking to a stranger about things so profoundly felt. So, while she sat out in the sunshine, she composed an email to Andrew.

*Dear Andrew,*

*I got your email, and I understand your impatience to be healed and back to normal. You are a man used to action, and it must be very frustrating to feel held back. I know your pain is severe, and I wish I could have helped you more. You're right to try something else –*

*I need to as well. I need to love nursing again. I need to see more babies born right now -- more simple cases. I'm glad you are so strong. You will succeed, and I will as well. We are on separate paths now but going in a positive direction. I admire your approach, and I hope it's what you expect. Please let me know if you need anything.*

Lily picked up the journal she'd brought outside to write on. She needed to start keeping a diary of her healing journey. Today she would. She'd look at her life differently – Of course, Fife was part of it, and the letter from Andrew solved a problem – having no urgent reason to return to the states – her contract job was for Andrew's rehab alone; it seemed she was at liberty to stay a bit longer.

That would give her some time to heal and explore her relationship with Fife. They hadn't ever lived on the same continent – let alone in their small town, but for a few vacations. Time to find out if the distance was the attraction or if being closer together would propel their relationship to new heights. Time to try out nursing again. But small-scale. Starting with the babies and gallbladder operations. Opening her MacBook laptop, she quickly went into Safari and pulled up an internet search for nursing positions on the Scottish isles. As long shots went by, it was a long one. With shaking hands, she googled "nursing jobs – Skye."

Three days later, she was hired as a temporary general nurse by the very grateful people at Portree Medical Center. But, *dear God, please don't let this be a mistake!* Lily thought out loud.

# CHAPTER 9

A ndrew had deliberately fired Lily. He knew she wanted the best for him, but he knew what that was. He needed a facility that would challenge him much more. His vision of healing included building his strength up to compensate for his missing limbs – not just adjusting to life without his legs.

Andrew's parents would do anything to help him. Even though he was a decorated cop and all 'hard edges,' Andrew was also a trust fund baby. His parents were very wealthy. They promised him access to any rehab facility he wanted. And he'd found the right one.

Within days of her departure, Andrew had found a rehab facility that promoted strength training and promised his wheelchair would no longer define him. They admitted that it would take time to bring him back but that their process would make him an athlete – someone who would transcend his injury.

Camp StandUP was a private rehab operated by Vince Conroy – a former Navy Seal who had rehabbed friends who'd lost limbs. He promised boot-camp-like workouts – a promise to get past the loss of limbs in 6 months. After that, he would walk and run with prostheses – climb mountains.

Andrew was confident that, given time, Conroy would give him the no excuses workout he needed. And with that time, he could also reconcile his heart to healing.

He was angry at the bombers, angry that one bomber died and the other was captured – that was his mission – to bring them to justice, and he was sure it wouldn't have been dainty. He was angry that his career as a cop was ended. He loved his job and liked that he could help people – but now Andrew didn't know that he could be that kind of cop again.

Hate swirled in his belly, and it fed itself during the hours that Andrew lay awake at night due to the phantom pain from his missing legs. For a time, Lily had encouraged him to pursue more positive thoughts – a step-at-a-time healing. But he knew in the days before Lily left that he couldn't do that work. And so, it was well that she went away.

Andrew didn't want her coming back because she would discourage this hard rehab. He'd tried to keep her involved because truth be told, he'd fallen for her. He couldn't picture anyone else by his side. But Lily had seen Andrew at his weakest. He didn't want her to carry that image with her. When they finally came together, they would be equals.

So, he sent her a note releasing her.

# CHAPTER 10

Having settled her immediate future, Lily felt better than she had in months. Tonight, Fife was coming back, and Lily was eager to tell him she could stay for a while. He couldn't possibly have expected this turn of events when he left nearly a week ago for the mainland. She assumed that he'd be willing to allow her to stay in the home he'd built, but she didn't want to presume; tonight, she'd ask him. Last night, Lily had spoken with Fife and asked him to come to dinner that night. Lily also knew that she owed it to Fife to tell him how she was healing.

He was a big, happy puppy, and he was a big part of her healing, but she wanted him to know about her guilt.

She'd put on some music and started a Boeuf Bourguignon. She wasn't much of a cook, but she did certain things well. Lily was looking forward to the cool nights of fall here on Skye. She loved sitting outside by the firepit that Fife had made, wrapped in a lovely soft throw – or wrapped up in each other. Lily wanted many more cozy romantic evenings with Fife before it was too cold to sit outside. In keeping with the comfort food theme, she'd bought a crusty baguette in town – suddenly missing her sister, a baker back in America.

And now, bubbling happily in the oven was an Apple Crisp.

The table was set with a meticulously pressed white cloth with the china and silver Fife had chosen. The lights were low, and the table was laden with candles and cloth napkins.

She'd set a Cabernet on the table and Waterford wine goblets at each place.

Coming back into the room after dressing, Lily was pleased with how cozy it looked, and, whimsically, she imagined the Aga smiled.

An hour later, dinner was ready, and still no Fife. Lily began to worry. Fife was never late. So, today was a mystery. She went to the little writing room and picked up the phone.

"Hello, Annis? Have you heard from Fife? I talked to him last night, and he was due for dinner here tonight – 1 ½ hours ago, actually

– and you know Fife, he's never late!" Lily tried to keep the rising panic from her voice.

"Lily – I just spoke with him. He is stuck on the ferry. His next call was going to be to you – he wanted to warn me first because I was picking him up. I imagine he's trying to call you now."

"Ok. I'll hang up then. Thanks for letting me know, Annis. I must admit I was beginning to panic."

No sooner had she hung the phone back on the hook; than it rang. "Lovely Girl! It is me, and I beg forgiveness. I took a later ferry than I expected because an inspection was slow. Hope I haven't ruined dinner!" Despite the time of day, Fife was just as light as always, and Lily was relieved he was ok.

"Are you coming here? I have dinner ready for you."

"Yes, mom will drop me off, and I'll walk home – unless you let me stay?"

"Let's just worry about dinner for now. How soon will you be here?"

"Probably no more than 45 minutes. Is dinner salvageable, or shall I get some fish and chips?"

"I turned off dinner an hour ago, so I will reheat it slowly. See you soon, my love." Lily bid him goodbye with a bit of a thrill.

# CHAPTER 11

10 pm

The dishes sat on the table, ignored for now, as Lily and Fife became reacquainted.

"Fife, stop. Now. I need to talk with you," Lily said sluggishly. She had been slowed down by Fife's leisurely kisses and by the wine of which she'd had more than a few glasses of. But the angel on her shoulder prevented the evening from proceeding. She knew that she needed to solidify her future with Fife first – but he a convincing argument.

"Dinner was wonderful, my love. I'm only sorry I was so late. But now that I've filled you in on my week, I would like to hear about yours." Fife drew away to the corner of the couch, acknowledging to himself that a bit of distance would help him focus better.

"Well, Fife, I hope you'll be happy to hear it -- I've taken a job here on Skye at the hospital. I wasn't prepared to do it so soon, but it seems Andrew has decided he doesn't need me anymore. I received a letter from him this week cutting me loose, and I spoke with my boss, who told me Andrew had checked himself out of the rehab. So, I'm spare gear now." Lily glanced at Fife, noticing that he was having difficulty restraining himself. But his attempt was valiant.

"Well, what do you think, Fife? Ok, for me to stay here for a while?" Her teasing was too much for him, and he fairly flew across from his perch on the couch and gathered her into his arms.

"Perfect! No problem. Let's plan the wedding! I'm ready to go, Lily. I would have married you 15 years ago. Am I to be rewarded now for that patience?" Fife was holding her so tenderly but so completely, Lily was almost unable to move, but she managed a turn and stretched up to kiss him softly on the chin.

"The timing isn't right, Fife. I need to find my way first. Andrew dumping me is good because it forces me to look at how I was affected by the bombings. I'm not whole yet – you know that! I still think about the brother dying on that table. I'm still glad he died - how, do you like that? How do you like the woman you want to marry being glad someone died? That isn't me. But I know that I love nursing, and I need to get back to it.

So, I found a job at the hospital part-time. I'm getting better, and it is in no small part because of you. I just need time before I make any other big decisions."

Lily watched the emotions play across Fife's face and could have predicted his next words.

"Lily. I will give you whatever time you need but let me hurry it along by saying the following: You tried to save that monster. You used all your skills. And you weren't alone trying – doctors and other nurses also failed. And, perhaps, it was inevitable that he died. His injuries resulted from his own actions – actually – his own bomb. Your gratitude for his death is natural – he was a monster and did monstrous things. Your reaction is a truth. It is not an indication you're unfit as a nurse. You worked hard to save him. You just couldn't. And you've lost other patients before – ones you thought you could save. Sometimes GOD steps in.

"Thank you, Fife. And I'm sure I'll get comfortable with that feeling once I've had a bit of time to settle down. And my love. I would love to marry you - eventually. But I need to do this work on my psyche first, and we will need time to plan the wedding properly. I want to have it here, but it may prove difficult for my family. So, let's think about it. And I want to make sure that our friends and your family can come easily as well. So, there's no rush."

And that was the last word spoken that evening.

# CHAPTER 12

The next few days sped by, with Lily settling herself in and preparing to work. Fife was busy and had to revisit the mainland because of some critical issues with the building site. Lily was disappointed he was leaving again – after all, he had just come back! She questioned him about if he had a supervisor who could take over.

"Lily, it's an issue with the supports on one section. Not surprisingly, that's the section where our sub-contractor was working when he quit a week ago—never working for me again! His work was sloppy, and I wish I'd never hired him.

I'm going to oversee the repairs. My name will be associated with the building, so I need to ensure it's perfect! I'll only be gone a few days. Edinburgh isn't that far away!"

"I know, Fife. I'll miss you, though. But unfortunately, when you come back, I'll have started my new job. I had hoped we could spend a few days together before that happened. But I'm only going to be working part-time, so I'll still be able to get you to myself on my day off!"

"That's right, love. I'm not going anywhere after that. Not until I get your promise to marry me sewn up!"

Lily kissed him goodbye with a passion that left Fife in no doubt about her affections.

# CHAPTER 13

By noon the next day, it was as if Lily had never taken a break from bedside nursing. The hospital was a small one with less than 50 beds. There was a children's ward with only two occupants that day; a geriatric ward with eight patients, and a maternity ward with three expectant moms and one who gave birth overnight. Lastly was the general ward, filled with medical and surgical patients, which today was blessedly empty.

There were three other nurses on with her – Jeannie, a plump, happy woman, who the kids in the pediatric ward adored; Lois, a silent, disapproving head nurse; and Amy.

Amy was cute and efficient and always seemed to be there when you needed her.

None of the patients seemed to be in desperate condition, and the morning was spent with the 'lovely elderlies' – Jeannie's term and Lily could see how right she was.

They were all so sweet – six women and two men. They cooed over her and wanted to know all about her. In particular, there was Joe. Joe Fitzgerald, he'd introduced himself. He was a farmer born on Skye, but 'he'd had a big job for years until he found that Skye was the antidote for the greed and anger uptown.' Joe had given up his job for a herd of Highland Cows.

Joe, who was 80 if he were a day, was hospitalized because one of his herd stepped on his foot and broke it.

He was a smallish man with an angular face and soft, cloudy eyes, which Lily sensed was because of cataracts. As she talked to him, Joe held her hand with one hand and patted it with his other. The Scottish brogue he spoke with doing more to soothe her nerves than the 45 minutes of yoga the night before. His voice sounded like he was telling her a fairy tale.

"Joe, I must get to work! Can't trade any more secrets with you today. But I will be back tomorrow, and we'll talk then." Lily gently unwound her hand from his surprisingly strong one.

"Tomorrow, bring that Fife with you. I want to ask him about Annis. She was a lovely lass back in school." Joe was smiling.

# CHAPTER 14

Sunday afternoon, while she sat outside on the patio, she put the radio on to the local Edinburgh station. She was determined to make Skye her home and decided that the only way was to absorb the culture. She chuckled when the first song that came on was Elvis' "Fool's Rush In." But in seconds, she was distracted by breaking news.

*"An explosion has rocked a construction site in Edinburgh. The blast caused a collapse of the southern corner of the Bank Street building. "The Bank Street Collection is the latest project from McCormack Construction. We understand that there was a dispute yesterday between the owner, Fife McCormack, and a former employee. It isn't known whether this explosion is related to that matter. Unfortunately, we are unable to interview McCormack at present."*

The reporter signed off, and all Lily was aware of was a buzzing in her head – the feeling of being unable to breathe and her hands going limp. Pushing through – she knew it was necessary now, Fife was in danger – she wouldn't, couldn't think about the prospect that he was dead. Just in danger. That's all.

*She wondered if Annis knew. How would she tell her if she didn't know? She didn't have to wait long to find out. Above her on the gravel drive, a car stopped short.*

"Lily. Lily, are you here? Lily?"

Lily heard Annis' voice but couldn't respond. Instead, she heard her knocking on the hen house door and was frozen in place because she was sure that Annis was coming to tell her Fife was dead.

"Lily! There you are. Didn't you hear me calling? Annis looked puzzled.

"Oh, you've heard. Haven't you? I tried to get here to tell you myself." Annis recognized that Lily wasn't completely together.

She reached out and held her, and Lily melted into her. And the sobbing began.

"We were going to be so happy. We were going to marry. And now it's done." Lily managed to choke out into Annis' shoulder.

"What do you mean it's done? We don't

know how he is. We haven't heard yet. But I knew after your recent trauma that you needed me here to wait with you. He'll be fine. You know, I can feel it in my heart. My heart doesn't feel torn. Just a bit bruised. He'll be fine." Annis kept repeating those words and could feel Lily quiet.

"Annis. I can't wait here. I need to go to him. Whatever the situation is, I need to see him. Will you go with me?"

"Of course, Lily."

# CHAPTER 15

Getting into Edinburgh was made much easier by Graham, Fife's best friend. Graham had flown Fife over in a rush a few days ago and now volunteered to take Annis and Lily.

Not knowing Lily's recent experiences, he repeated the news reports he'd heard over the morning; "3 dead for sure – It wasn't a bomb but a gas explosion. The neighborhood was evacuated. No record of how many were in the building when it exploded."

Lily heard everything, but she'd decided to hold off on worry and replay their last moments -- Fife holding her gently, telling her that he'd be home to marry her as soon as she'd have him. Fife describing their family – two redheads – a boy, and a wee lass. He'd held onto names over his lifetime and knew he wanted the boy to be named Finn and his daughter would be Esme. They'd have the boy first because Finn would be older and protect Esme from the monsters in school. He wanted to expand the henhouse so that the kids could have their own rooms right away and explained that he had a plan for that.

As they hovered over Edinburgh, Lily and the others could see the destruction. It seemed that the entire left side of the indoor mall had collapsed. Graham put the helicopter down on a local landing spot and helped them out.

As they made their way to the site, Lily was aware of a tightness in her chest. She wanted to rush ahead but couldn't because a sense of overwhelming loss held her back and made her struggle to breathe. She stopped a moment, allowing Annis and Graham to move ahead, and she felt like she was back in the hospital on that terrible day. Lives were lost, and the injured were all around her. She flashed back to the little girl that 'needed more Band-Aids' and the Cullen brothers whose lives would never be the same. And she thought about Andrew. What could have been. What never would again.

And she began to sob, with each sob releasing some of the tightness in her chest. She wept for all those others and for Fife and her and a marriage that may never be. She sobbed as she couldn't during those horrible days months ago. And she crouched on the sidewalk across from the building where she expected Fife was buried, consumed by sobs. A crowd began to gather around her.

"Lass, what's wrong? Are you ill?" The policeman's gentle voice prodded her.

"Lily, there you are – love, are you ok?" Annis' voice was strong and compassionate.

"Oh, Annis, he's gone! My lovely, loving Fife is gone. What'll I do now?" Lily sobbed as her heart broke.

"Not gone, love. Right here" A familiar voice answered her plea, and strong arms gathered her up. "Shush, love. I'm ok – we're all ok. The building imploded due to poor construction, not a gas leak, not a bomb. And we were all outside. Just some minor injuries. We're ok."

Fife's husky voice showed the strain of the last several hours and his worry on finding Lily in such a state. "Shush, love."

Lily, safe now and grateful to God that Fife wasn't hurt, hugged him tight. Her sobs now gone.

"Fife. I'm sorry for the dramatics. I flashed back to the bombing. I saw so much loss then, and I couldn't cry. The thought that I could have lost you was all just too much for me. It was just the next brick to fall."

"I think you may be suffering from a bit of post-traumatic stress. I want you to see someone when we get home." Fife said, concern in his voice.

"I will, Fife. I will."

Fife had to stay behind in Edinburgh to talk with the authorities and plan the cleanup. So, Graham brought Lily and Annis home.

# CHAPTER 16

**B**ack at the hen house, Annis saw Lily settled. Lily refused any food but had a cup of tea. Annis helped her to bed when she finished and stayed by her side until she fell asleep.

Annis stayed all night. She wanted to make sure that Lily was recovered from yesterday before she went home.

\* \* \* \* \*

"Good morning, Annis. Did you stay here all night? I'm ok. I have to work tomorrow, and my first job today is to find a therapist here on Skye. Do you know one?" Lily said, her tone subdued.

"I do have a good friend who'll come to you. Her name is Marjorie Stratton. She specializes in post-traumatic stress. I put a call into her last night, and she'll meet you here at ten this morning." Annis agreed with her son that Lily needed help.

"Thank you, Annis. She sounds perfect." Lily answered. "I have to get myself ready to work tomorrow."

"Do you think that's wise, Lily? Yesterday you had a trauma. Should you be putting yourself back in the hospital atmosphere?"

"Annis. Nursing has been my life for a long time. I need to find a way to get back to it. I think here on Skye is a good place to start. I've thought about it. I even woke this morning thinking about whether it was smart to give it up for now. What I know is that I will have lost a part of myself. I don't want to do that. Fife and I talked about how healing is part of my purpose. That I did my job back in Boston that week and that I can't save everyone. That I need to confront my work to move beyond it."

"Ok, sweetheart. I will leave you with that, and I hope that Marjorie will help you. I'll go now. Call if you need anything." Annis picked up her purse and moved toward the door.

"Thank you, Annis."

Lily looked at her watch and saw that it was nearly 9 am. *Time for a bath,* she thought. *Pull yourself together, gal.*

The bath helped.

She lingered a bit, thinking about yesterday and realizing she'd had a catharsis. She knew events still wounded her, but she also knew she could recover it. As she left the bath and wrapped herself in a towel, the phone rang,

"Fife? Oh, I'm so glad it's you. How are you? How's it going?"

"Hi, love. I'm exhausted, but the investigators have cleared me. The collapse was directly tied to the shoddy quality of the sub-contractor I mentioned. He's being charged and will be held responsible. It's a relief to me. That's not how I want my work to be thought of – thank God no one was seriously hurt. How are you? I was so worried about you yesterday." Fife's voice resonated with worry and exhaustion.

"I am ok today. I have a meeting with a therapist that your mother recommended in 20 minutes, and I'm looking forward to starting to heal. I am very sorry about my reaction yesterday. But I think it was cathartic. I feel lighter today. When are you coming home?"

"Tomorrow. We're cleaning up the debris field today, and I'll come home to plan the rebuild. I should be home by 3." Fife was looking forward to holding Lily again.

"Ok – I'm working from 7 to 3 tomorrow, so I'll be right behind you. Are you coming here or to your house?"

"I'm coming to you. I need to see you and hold you. Then I can sleep. Right now, what fills my dreams is you crying."

"Come here, and I'll hold you," Lily said with a hoarse voice.

# CHAPTER 17

The next day, near sunset, cuddled together on the patio, Fife and Lily set about healing each other.

"I met with Marjorie, and I think she'll be very helpful. I liked her approach. She treated me like a good friend who was having a hard time. Not clinical, just like talking to a friend. I felt much better after we talked, and we will meet again over tea here on the patio."

"And how was work? Do you feel comfortable there?" Fife asked, concerned for her work at the hospital.

"It was fine. I like the atmosphere there. And as for the medical side of it – very calm. No tragedies, just broken bones, and blood tests."

"I'm glad, but you must tell me if it becomes hard for you. You don't need to work

– you know that. So, whatever is best for you, I'm all for." Fife adored her and wanted her safe.

"Fife, talk to me about the building collapse. Now I know you and everyone else is safe; I want to know how you're feeling about it." Lily saw the exhaustion in his eyes. And she knew the pride he took in his construction jobs. This collapse must have devastated him.

"Lily, I want that man, Ron Crump of Crump Foundations, jailed. He lowballed his estimate, and I should have known better, but his answers made sense when I asked him about it. It seems they used sub-par rebar and their cement footings were the wrong mix. Fortunately, the authorities recognize where the error occurred and are pursuing charges against him. Luckily, I have built other buildings in Edinburgh, and they're familiar with my quality control. So, I don't think my reputation will suffer."

"I'm glad to hear that, honey, because I need some time with you. I realized yesterday that the one thing I'm sure of in my life is that I need you in it. So, if it's still on offer, I'd love to marry you. Soon.

"YES! She said YES!" Fife shouted.

"Hush! They'll hear you in Portree!"

"Portree will be thrilled. They adore you too!"

Fife, over the moon with happiness, pulled Lily in with the most loving of kisses, which Lily ardently returned, dissolving into their passion for each other.

# CHAPTER 18

L ily woke at nine with the feeling of being watched. There, sitting beside her – in a rumpled t-shirt was the man she was going to marry – Fife holding a steaming cup of coffee. She moved to slide out of bed but was cautioned by Fife.

"My love, stay where you are. I'll get your robe while you drink this coffee." Lily gratefully took the coffee from Fife, for it seemed she was dressed in nothing but her undies.

"Fife, did we, uh, you know?" she managed to squeak out.

"Ah, no, we didn't, but we did sleep together, and I promise I wasn't a complete angel – nor were you. There's time for the rest of it. We have our lives ahead of us." Fife said, unable to hide the seductiveness in his voice.

"Well, then. Thanks for the robe. Would it be too wanton of us to sit out on the terrace in our present attire?" Lily was embarrassed but also emboldened. She was going to marry this funny, sexy, handsome man, and she almost couldn't believe it.

"The chickens will be the only ones who'll see. So come with me, love, and bring your coffee."

The sun was warm on them but not as warm as it would have been back home. Scotland was cooler by 15 or 20 degrees from what Lily was used to. But in comparison to the hot summers at home, the temps here promised a summer of sweet romantic moments like this one.

"Let's talk wedding plans, my darling. I was thinking about it all night, I'm afraid." Lily was still foggy headed as a result. "How are we going to manage a wedding here and accommodate my family and friends or, conversely, your family if we held the wedding in Boston?"

"I tossed and turned, and at about four in the morning, the answer came to me and forced me awake! I would like a small ceremony here for my family, and then we could have the main wedding in the US. Mom, of course, would come along." Fife was triumphant in finding a solution. His main worry -- that time searching for the right answer would delay the wedding and give Lily time to back out.

"Perfect! Fife! That's it! No one will be left out. The people here are family to me now, too. What day should we choose?" Lily was excited and exhilarated to start a new life with Fife.

"Well, lovey, I would say this Saturday for our ceremony here, but I know you'll be wanting all the frills and the perfect location. So, let's make a list. Then, see what needs doing." Fife could hardly disguise his delight. This woman, the woman he'd loved for 15 years, unabashedly, would now be his wife very soon.

Fife felt like he'd won the lotto.

His life hadn't always been good – but his positive attitude after returning from Afghanistan seemed to bring out the best in karma. His life wasn't perfect – something had always been missing. And now that loop had closed.

"Come inside, and we'll get the list going. Then, perhaps, since I agreed to marry you, you could make me some eggs while we plan…" Lily teased.

# CHAPTER 19

An hour later, they had a plan. Annis had been notified ((officially) because she already knew of Fife's campaign to get Lily to the altar).

Now to notify her family. Of course, as it was early in the morning back in the states, they'd have to wait a while. But she knew one person who'd be up – her sister Lulu, the baker.

Lulu was as excited as Lily even though neither she nor any other member of the family had met him; Fife was well believed to be the perfect man for Lily – her soulmate.

And Lulu and the rest of Lily's family were worried she'd fall into a depression after the events of the last several months. "He sounds like the perfect man, Lily – a hulking Scot!" Lulu commented.

"Well, there has to be a more favorable term than hulking – he isn't a beast but a gentle giant.

I want you guys to get to know him before I marry him. Can you organize a get-together, and we'll skype in for the party? Just give me time to tell Mom and Dad. They deserve to hear from me directly."

"Oooh, that's a good idea – a skype interrogation by the siblings! Let me get that plan together, and then I'll let you know the date and time."

Lily chuckled as she hung up the phone. She knew Lulu and her other brothers and sisters would have only her best interests at heart. But the Griffins could be merciless!

Fife had wandered off to the Garden Lounge to make a phone call of his own. Very nearly beside himself, he knew that there was one person he needed to tell this news to on his own. He had kept a relationship with Anna's mother and her twin sister ever since Anna died. Now only Emma, Anna's twin, was still alive. She had been broken by her sister's death, much as Fife had. But she coped differently. The loss of the other half of herself had driven Emma into a strange world. She recognized her mother, and she recognized Fife. Her world was small but not rational. In it, her sister was a fairy gone off to fairylands.

And Fife had stayed behind to protect Emma and her mother. Emma lived in a small community home on Skye, taken care of by nuns. Fife knew that he needed (for himself) to tell Emma of his upcoming marriage. Of course, it would mean nothing to Emma, but because she was like a sister to him and he felt loyalty to Anna still, Fife wanted to tell her.

Even though Anna was his first love, his love for Lily was so much more. Not the first blush of youth, but a mature deep connection and an easy glimpse of the future. Lily was the left to his right and the beat of his heart. Fife knew the day he met her that they would end up at this place. And, while he mourned the circumstances that brought her here to him, he was grateful she'd had a reason to come.

After 14 years of loving her from afar, Fife decided he needed to make a move to something permanent last year. So, he began his restoration project on the henhouse. It grew out of hand and became like something one would call a 'folly'- it wound and jutted. Every room was a tribute to something he loved about Lily. The old-fashioned kitchen, with the homey table and furnishings; the quick little study with the wind blowing in full of warmth and sunshine; the little room full of china that just existed to be charming. They would make their home here and, with luck, fill it with babies. But, he knew they were getting on to an age where babies were less likely. And that was the thing that really lit a fire under him to get on with it. He hadn't thought whether Lily wanted children, and at that moment, he had a clench in his gut, worrying she wouldn't. But, they'd cross that bridge when they came to it.

# CHAPTER 20

That evening, Annis held a Ceilidh and welcomed nearly the entire village to celebrate the engagement of Lily and Fife. Bagpipes were played near the open door by Brodie. Meath and the sound carried across Portree Harbor.

Although there would be a wedding to come, the villagers who'd raised Fife and supported him through all that drama years ago – had helped him recover himself after his time overseas; wanted to see him happy and settled finally – and that meant no one for him but Lily. And so, there was much joy that night.

\* \* \* \* \* \*

Annis, who had thought of Lily as a daughter for 15 years, was relieved that Fife would now be confident in Lily's love. And Lily would be here, safe in this little village so far away from danger. But, while Annis knew that the bubble, they lived in was unusual, every time Lily went back home, she worried, and she feared for her son Donal and his family in New York as well. The world had turned a corner with the century and brought anger and terror along with innovation.

Right now, looking at Fife with Lily, Annis could convince herself that all was well in the world. Right now.

\* \* \* \* \* \*

Fife held Lily in his arms and danced slowly to a familiar Scottish waltz, feeling a happiness he hadn't felt for close on 18 years. When Anna died, a part of Fife had as well. He had grown up with her, and they had been destined for each other since they were wee babies. So, when she died in her sleep on her 18th birthday, Fife was devastated. His purpose was lost.

He wandered for months, wondering if living were preferable to the crushing sense of loss he felt. He wasn't entirely sure himself, so he joined the Royal Regiment of Scotland and was soon deployed to Afghanistan. Two bloody tours of duty there taught him that he did indeed want to live, and he did have a further purpose. As a medic, the men he couldn't save were like a promise he made to live life to the fullest. Coming home after his last deployment, he found a new purpose and pursued building his fledgling construction company so that it could support one pro bono project a year – a children's home, a rec center, a hospital wing. Things were good for him, but he didn't ever breathe a happy breath until he encountered Lily on a trail.

He squeezed her now, remembering. She was but a speck of dust compared to his Brobdingnagian build, but she felt right in his arms, and she squeezed back. Life was beginning for them anew.

\* \* \* \* \* \*

Lily acknowledged that life was good now, but there was a hesitancy in her that she couldn't put her finger on. She knew she loved Fife and knew he was the right man for her, but there was a discomfort Lily felt whenever she acknowledged to herself how lucky she was. That patch of time back in Boston was receding the longer she was with Fife. He had such a way of making her feel comfortable and safe, and loved. Lily knew that the path she was now on was the right one. Then, of course, she worried about being so far from family, but her loved ones and friends were only as far away as the internet these days.

She pushed her discomfort aside – and focused on the dreamy night that had her thinking about the wedding – the one at home. *Would everyone be able to come? And what needed to be done for the one here – less than a week away?*

# CHAPTER 21

Between Midnight and 2 am, Fife and Lily planned the wedding on Skye.

The service would be in a church on the hilltop overlooking the harbor, and there would be a simple reception afterward. Fife would have stayed the night, but Lily reminded him that they were only days away from having forever together. They could wait. Fife agreed, reluctantly, taking his leave at 2:30. Lily fell asleep, where she sat on one of the cozy couches in the Garden Lounge.

In the morning, Annis came to take Lily on a shopping trip. Of course, a proper wedding dress was required, and she knew just the shop. But Lily was hesitant and a bit weirded out by a dream that had woken her shortly before 6.

"Listen, Annis, I'm a traditional girl, but I'll look ridiculous in lace. So, let's just get a plain white dress and be done with it."

"Ridiculous in lace? How do you figure that? Your face and figure are a bridal dream. You're going to look gorgeous." Annis said in disbelief.

"I don't know. I just feel like it's a bit over the top. You know my life has been very dramatic over the past several months. Don't you think a more subtle gown is called for?" Lily explained somewhat haltingly.

"Lily, do you not want this marriage? Of course, it's not entirely too late – but if you're going to avoid breaking my son's heart - you should do it soon. Fife is determined to marry you, and I've never seen him happier."

"Annis. I do want to marry Fife. I guess I'm just embarrassed by overtly celebrating when I know so many people who have been killed and injured in the last six months. Marjorie is helping me to deal with all that, but it'll take some time.

This island is so far away from all that, and that's why I feel safe here. It's easy to forget, I suppose." Lily knew that she had to level with Annis, though the dream the night before was almost too real.

"Can we have a cup of tea before we leave? I'd like to talk with you."

"Of course, love. It's a beautiful day – let's sit outside." Annis answered, glad that it seemed Lily was going to open up to her.

The two women took their steaming mugs and walked out to the overlook where Fife had built their patio. The sun was warm, and Lily sat for a moment, hypnotized by a hummingbird hovering over the garden.

After a moment, Lily was calmed and, after a refreshing sip of her tea, opened up to Annis.

"Annis, I love Fife very much, you know that, but last night I dreamt of him dying. I dreamt that as I was walking down the aisle, a bomb blew up in the front of the church.

Fife was in a million pieces, and I couldn't put him together again. He was the only one. The only one who was hurt, and as I ran from the carnage outside, Andrew – the man I was nursing back in Boston, was standing there." Lily wept deep, shaking sobs.

"I couldn't imagine going on without Fife. And so, there, at the top of the hill outside that glorious church, I ran past Andrew and leapt off the cliff. Never to be without Fife." Lily's voice went hoarse.

Lily's dream shook Annis, but she had the advantage of clarity, and this very clearly was a trauma Lily must find a way to deal with.

"Lily. Lily. That was a dream, and you are obviously working out the trauma you faced in Boston in your dream. Have you talked with your therapist about this?"

"No. The dream was just last night, but I will on Wednesday when we meet. I just needed to talk it out this morning. Annis – Fife was killed. How do I reconcile that with working out the trauma?"

"Well, I'll tell you. Fife is the last thing you can stand to lose. He is the man you would follow to the edge of the world – right?"

"Right."

"And Andrew was waiting there to prove to you, you CAN put him back together, but you ran past. Why? Talk it through with me."

"I guess I didn't want Andrew to distract me from being with Fife. Andrew needed me for a long time, and now he doesn't, which makes it easier to be with Fife, but I feel like I ran away from Andrew, and I still worry about how he is. What does that say about me? Am I being disloyal to Fife? To Andrew? I'm not sure what my next step is in life."

"Exactly, Lily. You're having cold feet but also are diminishing your importance – you feel you don't deserve a lace wedding dress because you believe you ran away from Andrew, which makes you unworthy of Fife.

Let me tell you a few things. Andrew – you told me this yourself – Andrew sent you away. Didn't he leave the rehab and discharge you of your responsibility to him? Your trauma from those days hasn't been dealt with properly, and though they may not be as visible as the wounds Andrew and the others suffered, they ARE as dangerous. You need to get your confidence back. When do you work again at the hospital?"

"On Monday. In addition to the other departments that have a need, I'll be working in the ER again. I don't expect that I'll see the kind of injuries I'm most recently used to, but I'm still a bit nervous."

"Well, one day at a time. Each day will get easier, and your confidence in yourself will grow."

Annis recognized that Lily was healing and trying to figure it out. Time would tell.

"Let's go shopping."

# CHAPTER 22

Several hours later, Lily returned home with exactly what she had envisioned for a wedding dress – a white linen shift, unadorned except for a sprig of heather embroidered at the shoulder. It was dignified as befit the occasion but casual enough to be wearable again. And she also had made a decision about the Skye wedding. She just needed to discuss it with Fife.

Fife was due anytime because they were skyping with her family at home. So, it would catch many of them at Sunday breakfast, which was always a happy time for her family.

"Good afternoon, my love! T-minus 10 minutes until I meet your family. How do I look?"

He looked magnificent, her gorgeous Scot. Rusty hair combed to the side, freshly shaved, and smelling like lavender. His navy polo shirt opened at the neck, and muscles bulging the arms. His jeans fit him like they were made for him and as he smiled at her, his eyes twinkled, and she fell in love again today.

"Well, if you don't mind me saying – and don't let it go to your head – you're gorgeous and having a good hair day. My family will think you're too good for me," Lily replied.

"Ahhh, kind words, but I'm exactly good enough for you! I was made for you," Fife answered, his voice getting husky.

"Fife, before the call, I want to run an idea past you. I think the church is lovely and the overlook beautiful, but I've had a vision of you and me marrying in the heather. What do you think? After all, that's where we met."

"Brilliant. Perfect. I love the idea, and I know you have secretly wished for a simple ceremony. The only things I require are you, mum, and a priest. Now kiss me!"

Lily let the kiss go on almost too long. But by the time they opened the skype call, her hair was tousled and her cheeks bright pink.

"Scotland agrees with you, honey," her mother said with a twinkle in her voice.

"Yes, you look so much better. Where is

this Fife so I can thank him?" added her father in his trademark teasing voice. When she called them a few days ago, both of her parents were delighted to hear she was marrying Fife, but her dad warned her that he would like to see the man first. Now he was.

"Mr. and Mrs. Griffin – I'm Fife, and I'm so delighted to meet you that I beat Lily to the introduction! She's lovely, isn't she?"

"Yes, Fife, we think so. I'm Pete, her big brother."

"Oh, Pete! I feel like I know you already! Fife was immediately comfortable.

Without Lily even getting a word in edgewise, all the others introduced themselves and began to challenge Fife with questions, like "can you support her? She buys a lot of makeup, you know;" and "She's gonna make you go to France – just warning you." That, from Genie, her other sister (Genie was short for Regina – her mother wouldn't allow it to be shortened to Reggie.) They were a happy crowd together, and Lily began to feel homesick.

Her nieces and nephews were joining in as well. And everyone had a story about Lily.

"So, anyway, everyone, we were thinking of planning the wedding for September 1st. Can you mark it down?" Lily broke up the hazing of Fife. Griffins were loud. Better for Fife to find out now, although he was like a big loveable puppy, so she knew he would fit right in.

"September 1st? You're not getting married until September 1st? We have plenty of time," Genie added – clearly already in planning mode.

"Well, we are having a small ceremony on Saturday here for Fife's friends – err ... my friends and family. So, technically we'll be married when we come home. We know that isn't ideal, but we couldn't bring all of you here, nor could we bring all our loved ones here, home. I hope you don't mind." Her parents knew already, and they were ok with it; although Lily knew her dad was disappointed at not being able to walk her down the aisle, but there was nothing else they could do.

Despite the pangs of homesickness, she'd felt at the beginning of the call, Lily was rejuvenated by the time with her family. Any worry she may have had about how they'd receive Fife was erased after her brothers quizzed him and wanted to include him on a bike ride when they got to the states. With loud goodbyes, the skype call ended.

"Fife, I think I can marry you now. They approve – although I'd marry you anyway!"

Lily added with a soft kiss on Fife's forehead.

"Grrrr! Come here, my love, and I will show you how lucky you'll be to have me." Fife said as he grabbed her around the waist and pulled her down to his lap.

"I can only just wait to Saturday to make you mine. So, here's something I'm wondering about – how will your new job handle a honeymoon in your second week?"

"Well, I've been wondering about that too, and I wonder if I made a mistake taking this job." It was something else that Lily had been worrying about recently.

"You know I can support you, my love. But, if you decide it's going to be too much until after the wedding, put it off. I know the head man over at the hospital – I'd be happy to put a word in for you. Or don't work at all. What would you do if you didn't work? What is your passion? Would you paint, write?"

"I need to work, Fife. I don't need the money. I gave notice to my landlord, so my rent is paid on the apartment, and my sisters and brothers are cleaning it out for me. My car has been returned to the dealer. It was leased, and I've turned it in early. My other bills are low, and I can pay them with my savings, so money isn't an object. I need to feel useful. And, to me, usefulness is all about looking after people's health. I can work there, and if they object to the time off I need, I'll find something else after the weddings." Having now talked it all through - first her anxiety with Annis and then the practicalities with Fife, Lily felt a distinct lessening of tension.

"Then come to the heather with me, my love, and let's find the perfect location for our wedding!"

# CHAPTER 23

L ate that afternoon, Lily bid Fife goodnight. She wanted to be rested before work the next day. And she had decided to go back to yoga to center herself. Lily had been a practitioner of yoga for years until that spring. It had always helped her shake off the worst parts of her job.

She would spend some time with yoga, have a light meal, and tuck into bed with a book.

Fife was going up to London for the next few days for work, so he didn't have any problem with an early night.

# CHAPTER 24

"Get up, Andrew! Get up! You know you can. No excuses!" Conroy berated Andrew, who'd fallen during a training session.

The first time Andrew fell this morning, Conroy helped him up. Told him how to use canes and his upper body strength to propel himself standing. The second time he didn't. Andrew had to learn how to use his prostheses himself.

It was humiliating. He was left helpless on the floor, literally floundering to get to a standing position. He wished he'd focused on Conroy's instructions the first time. Now, Conroy was standing, yelling commands at him, demoralizing him, angering him.

Andrew wanted to scream. He had been screaming in his head now for months. Before the bombing, he was a cop with a record of accomplishments. He was in line to be a captain in the time before the bombing. Andrew was going to get married. Now, none of that was happening. Instead, he'd been pensioned off the force. And Melissa had moved on when she realized that Andrew's injuries were so severe. No life for her as a nurse--she would leave that to the professionals.

So, Andrew was left alone.

Alone to fight the bogeyman that was his life. And the only person who understood; the one person definitely in his corner was Lily, and he'd sent her away.

Conroy was tough and delivered exactly what he promised; he would walk again on his mechanical legs if he could just get himself off the floor. And he would. Biting nearly through his lip, he dragged himself up in just the way that Conroy had taught him—no more going easy on himself. His recovery was tied to his self-esteem. And his self-esteem was tied to his strength and determination.

That's why he had been a good cop, and it was why he'd survive. But he knew that saving himself was a first step back to Lily.

# CHAPTER 25

The next few days flew by until suddenly, it was Thursday. Lily woke with a start to that news – two days until she married Fife! Two days until she and Fife made official their love for each other. She hadn't seen him for a few days because he had some business on the mainland that he wanted to get done before the festivities.

Lily thought about the next few days. The hospital had insisted she take tomorrow and Monday off for wedding preparations and a weekend honeymoon. It surprised her how quickly she'd become friends with her fellow nurses and the small administrative staff at Portree General.

So, today would be it until Tuesday, and Lily was grateful for that. The wedding, as requested, was taking place in a clearing of the heather where Fife and Lily had met. Fife told her that some of his crew were erecting a small altar and bringing folding chairs for the guests. Lily's thoughts were interrupted with a wish that her own family was represented, but they would see her married in September – but now Lily wondered if she could have someone include her parents in the service via Skype. She'd mention it to Fife later.

The reception after the wedding would take place in the village hall, and Annis and the other ladies in the village had been cooking all week. Sam, Fife's good friend, would take the photographs, and Megan, his wife, was preparing the wedding cake.

As she left the hospital, Lily thought about what she had to do. First, she was stopping in Portree to order the flowers. Then, tonight, she was to have dinner with Fife and his mom, Annis, to discuss the final details, and tomorrow was beauty day. Annis had made an appointment with a spa for a home massage, manicure, pedicure, and facial for Lily, and then it was early to bed for her. On Saturday morning Annis was coming at 9 to help her dress for the wedding.

As much as she loved Annis, Lily was sad her mother would not be there. There was that life-long image of her mother helping her into her dress, arranging her veil, and her dad walking her down the aisle. Lily knew that she'd have that when they married in the states – but this was the first one – the real one, and she wanted her folks there to share it.

Forcing her thoughts away, she wondered if Fife was back from his trip. She worried when he wasn't around. Finally, she decided she would call him as soon as she finished with the flowers.

Heather and white roses were the only flowers she wanted, and fortunately, the florist could accommodate. So, she decided on a spray of heather with one white rose for Fife; a bouquet of white roses for herself and mixed heather and roses for Annis. It would be lovely and just simple enough for the wedding she'd planned.

Exiting the flower shop, she had calling Fife on her mind and was looking in her bag for her phone when she walked directly into him.

"Whoa, Nellie! What's the rush? No time for a little kiss?" Fife said, wrapping his arms around her warmly.

"Fife! You're home! I was just going to call you! I'm so happy to see you." And, with that, proceeded to deliver a kiss to Fife that left him in no doubt that she'd missed him.

"Well, we should be hurrying that wedding along. I can't wait for the honeymoon, and I don't think you can, either." Fife drew away and looked down at the woman who'd redefined living for him. He would give everything he had to protect her and keep her by his side. He vowed that she would never be unhappy with him if he could prevent it.

"Come along. I'll drive you home. Mom's bringing dinner, so no need to do anything else. Have a tub; read a bit."

"Sounds lovely."

The first thing that Lily noticed as they pulled up in front of her little (or not so little) hen house was the curtains flying in and out of the windows. And the door was ajar – a bag blocking the way. Her pulse began to race a bit – knowing that she hadn't left it that way at just before 7 am when she'd left for work. Now, it was after four, and it couldn't have been open all that time.

"Fife, she said warily, the door is open, as are the windows. Something isn't right. Have you been in and out of the henhouse today?"

"No, my love, but I am certain that it is nothing to be worried about. Skye is safe. Perhaps someone dropped off a wedding gift and forgot to close the door. Let's see."

Lily was a little let down that Fife wasn't concerned. He reached out and helped her from his jeep and pulled her along to the house. "Fife, …. Fife, shouldn't we call the police?" Lily asked, a tremble becoming evident in her voice.

"Ach, it's fine. Perhaps it's me, ma. T'will be fine," said a very unconcerned Fife.

They were at the front door now, and the bag propping the door seemed to be a familiar-looking piece of luggage. Then, just as she was reaching to push the bag out of the way, an arm grabbed it from her, and Lily was facing her father.

"Dad! You're here! For my wedding? Thank you! Is Mom here too?"

"Yes, honey, I am, answered her mother from behind her dad. And don't thank us – Fife emailed us a few days ago that he thought you'd want your parents at the wedding; he sent us tickets and collected us at Heathrow. Since our flight was delayed, we didn't get in until yesterday afternoon, so Fife put us up at the Four Seasons Park Lane and took us to dinner last night. Where is Fife?"

Lily looked and saw the jeep just driving away. Fife was giving them time alone. What a great guy she was getting.

"Honey, HE is a great guy," her dad said, echoing her thoughts. "He spared no expense and was the warmest and most charming of hosts. I think he was trying to impress us. And it worked."

# CHAPTER 26

The next day was a girl's day, so Fife took Lily's dad to the highlands for a manly hike.

Although she worried about how her 'older' dad would do hiking, Lily knew she needn't worry with Fife in charge. He'd never risk the life of his future father-in-law.

It was nice for Lily to have time alone with her mother before Annis got there. They talked quietly in the outside sitting area about everything. Her mom loved Fife already, as did her Dad. They were happy she was settling down from the tragic spring she'd had. And as her oldest daughter was marrying, there was a sigh of satisfaction to see her settled and so very happy.

"Mom, I have a confession to make. I am supposed to be writing my vows today, and I don't know where to start. Any ideas?" Lily asked.

"What do you love most about Fife, Lily," her mother replied.

"Mom, he takes me out of myself, puts everything in perspective for me. He is joy and laughter, love, and warmth. He makes me feel safe and special. He is the man I always dreamt of. He is the man I want to father my children, although I haven't asked him about that yet."

"There, my darling, are your vows. Well, except about the fathering children thing. That should be a private conversation."

Carol and Tom Griffin were thrilled with Fife, especially given the two young people's long courtship. Distance dating was not a thing to be recommended, but Fife and Lily's relationship seemed to thrive on it. For several years now, the Griffins had been waiting for the wedding. And now it was here.

Lily had always been shy but strong. As a nurse, she dealt with the worst that life handed out and the best. The babies were her favorite. But working in an inner-city hospital had its' burdens, and never more so than the terror attack, this year. Carol worried that Lily was marrying because of her experience this spring. But seeing how she glowed here convinced Carol that this marriage was right, and Lily was home.

She'd said as much to her husband, Tom, last night after dinner with their soon-to-be son-in-law and his mother. They were jolly and happy, and Lily seemed to blossom under their attention.

# CHAPTER 27

One more set of reps, Andrew, and I'll let you go. Focus on your goal. It's right there."

"She's right there." Andrew corrected him.

The sweat washed over him. He'd been working solidly since sending Lily on her way. He knew this rehabilitation would be ugly, and he wanted to do it on his own. But unfortunately, Lily had become too personal to him. His gratitude to her had turned into a crush at his darkest time -- when she wouldn't let him give up – knowing more than Andrew did about what he was capable of.

Andrew knew it was difficult on Lily. He'd seen it in her eyes from the first moment he'd met her in the ER. She was stoic, but he saw the heartbreak in her eyes as she viewed his injuries.

Andrew wanted to do something about it, but back then, his only goal was recovery and retribution. And, unbelievably, there was no one left to pursue. The teenager was in jail, and his brother, dead. So, his only goal now was healing Lily's heartbreak.

# CHAPTER 28

As Lily lay in the bath that night, having been combed and cut, buffed and polished and massaged every which way, Lily felt a sense of peace like nothing she'd felt before.

Tomorrow she would marry a man she'd loved for more than a decade and in whom she'd found her best friend. Life was perfect. And tomorrow night, Fife and Lily would honeymoon in this lovely home Fife had built for her. Her parents were moving to Anise's house for a day or two before returning home.

Suddenly it occurred to her that she and Fife had not discussed something fundamental. She got out of the tub and wrapped in a towel, quickly called Fife.

"Lily? Lily, what are you doing calling in the middle of the night before our wedding?"

Fife sounded surprised and a bit wary. "You're not dumping me, are you?"

"Fife. No, of course not. But we haven't talked seriously about something fundamental, and I don't want to be married until we are on the same page. Do you want children? Because I do, and I don't have that many years to do it. I'm 35, so it could be too late if I don't get pregnant soon. And I've realized I don't know how you feel about kids." Lily's voice trailed off.

"Here I was thinking how lucky I was to have you and worrying about the same thing. Yes. I want children with you, desperately. I want a little girl who is the image of the brave, strong, shy, and loving you. I want a boy I can teach to fish and for whom I can build a treehouse. I spend nights lying in bed picturing our children, and I had a moment of fear yesterday that you didn't share that vision.

Yes. I'm in a rush for children, and I suggest we get started tomorrow!" Fife said almost too loudly for the middle of the night.

Lily blushed, and her throat closed. "It's a date." And she quietly shut off the phone.

# CHAPTER 29

"Do you, Fife Alan McCormack, take Lily Ellen Griffin to wed?" intoned Pastor Stevens in a very somber tone.

Lily wondered why he treated marriage as such a dull affair – it should be sounded like fireworks and fairy bells. The pastor should be proclaiming his excitement to marry two such in-love people.

Lily, herself, was soaring. Her insides were doing summersaults, and she couldn't prevent the hand Fife held from shaking. Fife was seemingly somber - except when he raised his downcast eyes - then Lily could see a twinkle in them.

Thankfully, the pastor was almost finished, and it was Lily and Fife's turn for vows.

Lily's summersaults became more

intense, and she was aware that her mouth was dry. Suddenly the guests and the pastor were quiet. "Lily?" she heard Fife as quietly.

She snapped out of her reverie, took a deep breath, and spoke.

"Fife, more than fifteen years ago, you rescued me from a fall, not so very far from here. Our friendship was instantaneous, but over the years, I have fallen in love with you and your booming laugh, your early cautious kisses, the way your heart quiets mine when you hug me and how my hands feel empty when they aren't holding yours'. I wish we'd married 15 years ago, but I will give you the rest of my life." The tears that had built in her eyes overflowed gently, and Fife traced them down her face before speaking.

"Lily. Your heart quiets to mine because you're my soulmate, and I am yours. When I found you on that hill where you fell, I had been thinking about the hole missing in my heart. And now that hole is full. You have made my heart full. And, you have come home."

"Lily and Fife, by expressing your vows in such an open and emotional way, we share in your love, and we support you completely. Your words have sanctified your marriage and have proven to those gathered here that you not only belong together for eternity but that you have waited for each other. That wait is complete. So, by the power vested in me, I now pronounce you man and wife," the pastor intoned, now with true joy in his voice, "You may kiss the bride."

Fife beat the pastor to it.

# CHAPTER 30

Later that night, after the brief wedding reception, wrapped in the arms of her husband in a bath full of bubbles, Lily gave a start. "You know, I believe we said our vows without actually saying the words, "I love you" or "I do! So, just so there is no mistake, I DO! And I Love you!"

As she twisted around to kiss Fife again, he said, "I love you, Mrs. McCormack," and "I DO." Shall we get out of this tub and go to bed?"

"Mmmmm, yes, please, Mr. McCormack."

# CHAPTER 31

L ily woke to an empty bed and the smell of coffee and bacon. She allowed a slow, small smile to spread. My husband cooks…!

Ten minutes later, robed and with a washed face, Lily joined her husband, who was cooking in his boxers. Lily bit back a little chuckle – his boxers said, "Groom."

The table was set with her favorite china – blue and white and chipped with age. The white woven mats were complemented with dark blue cloth napkins, and in the center was a vase of red roses.

Lily squinted at something at her place – vision clearing; she realized that it was her heart stone, and the square depression was filled with a small rock just the right size and shape.

"You're right, my love, as she hugged him

from behind. We are soul mates – our hearts are now complete." "I love you, Mr. McCormack!"

Monday, when both of them had had enough of the hen house, Fife and Lily packed a lunch and set off on a walk. The highlands beckoned, and the sun shone down on their pale skin. But, while it felt good to get some 'other exercise,' Lily knew that she could now never sleep without Fife by her side. And Fife knew that no matter what else he had done in his life, nothing made him feel happier than having Lily beside him, forever.

Tomorrow it would be back to reality.

# CHAPTER 32

As the days went on, Lily and Fife developed a new routine. Lily was first out, but they would manage coffee together before she left for her 7 am shift at the hospital, and Fife left at 8. Once in the hospital, Lily would put her bag and phone in her locker and get to work. So, it was a complete surprise at the end of the first day to find that Fife had texted her every hour. "Miss you, Mrs. M." "I love you," and other romantic notes.

That night as they cooked dinner side-by-side, Lily said, "Fife, thank you for the love texts you sent today. I'm sorry I can't answer them, but I'm not allowed to have my phone with me at work."

"That's OK, love. I knew that. I just wanted you to know I was thinking about you." Fife added, kissing her on her cheek.

"I knew."

And daily, the texts continued.

Friday night, they had Annis to dinner. Her parents had left Monday afternoon but had enjoyed Annis' company so much that they had arranged for her to stay with them when Fife and Lily married stateside.

"While I'm in the US, I am going to spend a few weeks with Donal. He'll bring me to New York after the wedding." Annis mentioned while they were relaxing over coffee.

"I'm anxious to meet him – and his family," said Lily. She was glad that Donal was coming to the wedding for that reason, but also because she'd heard stories of pranks he'd pulled, (secretly she worried that he would pull one at the wedding). She'd mentioned something to Fife about it, and he'd assured her that Donal knew about appropriate timing. "It's a bit a release valve for him. He's a defense attorney, and he handles serious cases. So, I think he just needs some fun amid the dread."

# CHAPTER 33

On Saturday Lily, and Fife joined a Skype call to discuss wedding plans. There was only a month before that wedding, and much to do.

Naturally, Genie had plans well in hand, with assists from Lulu and Pete. Lulu was the practical one. Genie was the dreamer and designer, and Pete was the one who could be relied on for strength and keeping the plan going. Drew and Jack were involved, too – Drew was collecting them from the airport and getting them settled, and Jack was going to play music at the church.

Lulu took charge. "So, we have 79 for the reception. Genie booked the Boston Harbor Hotel at Rowes Wharf for that. You two are booked in there as well. Annis is staying with Mom and Dad – we'll get her there after we drop you off. Drew and I will meet you at the airport. We thought it would be nice to have a private harbor tour the next day, so Drew rented a private boat for us to take around the harbor and a lunch after on one of the islands – we thought we'd show you our island, Fife! The church – St Joseph's, is booked, and the rehearsal will be at four on Saturday. Then, Mom and Dad are having dinner at their house for the wedding party. I know you spoke with Patsy and Franny about being bridesmaids, and we have Donal and Pete as ushers."

"By the way," Genie broke in, "the nieces and nephews want a job, so they're taking you two out to breakfast on Saturday morning. Be ready!"

"Oh my God. I know that Donal's daughter, Melly, would love to be part of that –." "Already arranged," Pete interrupted. "I spoke with Donal about it last night. He and I are tight."

"Pete," Fife interjected. "Be very careful. Donal is a vicious practical joker, and if you're not careful, you'll find your tux exchanged for a small or your coffee laced with pepper. Nothing is sacred!"

"Fife, you told me that Donal won't play any jokes at the wedding. Do I need to worry?" Lily asked with laughing trepidation.

"He promised me," Fife swore.

"Jack's been practicing the Ave Maria," Genie mentioned.

"Oh, God! Are we all carrying hankies?" Lulu interrupted. It was well known that Lulu cried at every Ave Maria, which Catholics played at both weddings and funerals.

"Suck it up, Lulu! They'll be happy tears," Lily ended the teasing that had broken out among the Skypers.

# CHAPTER 34

Fife and Lily were surprised by a last-minute invitation to dinner with Annis – they were accustomed to dining with her once a week and tonight's invitation was not only off schedule, but mysterious. When Lily asked what the occasion was and if she could bring something, Annis became a bit flustered and said, "Why does it need to be an occasion – I just want to see you two!"

"Ok, well we're looking forward to it! See you later." Hanging up, Lily turned to Fife and said "Well, that was odd. If there was one characteristic of your mother that I would mention first – it's how direct she is. Just now, I think she was evading my questions."

"I just saw her yesterday, and she seemed fine. She was coming out of the beauty parlor, which is a bit different, because she normally doesn't fuss with her hair, but she was just as happy and smiley as always. Maybe it's our wedding gift…." Fife conjectured.

"Fife my love, she gave us those lovely cashmere throws for the winter lounge for our wedding gift. What else were you expecting?" Lily teased.

"I don't necessarily expect anything, but now you've made me very curious. Can't wait for dinner!" Fife answered.

# CHAPTER 35

That evening, all became clear. There were four of them for dinner. Annis had a date!

"Joe Fitzgerald, I haven't seen you since the hospital. It's amazing to see you here!" Lily said, glee and astonishment in her voice.

"Young Fife brought Annis to see me on one of your days off. She and I hit it off! Just like back in school."

"We have been stepping out a bit with each other," Annis admitted, a blush creeping up along her cheeks.

Lily looked over at Fife to see a very self-satisfied smile on his face. So like Fife. She'd ask him later why he hadn't told her about his matchmaking.

Joe was still on crutches, so at dinner, Annis helped him to the table with a soft arm around him (and from Lily's perspective – it was a bit more of an embrace than a helping hand.)

Dinner was so much fun! It was clear that Joe and Annis were perfect for each other and their long-ago history was the start of something much more permanent – if delayed.

# CHAPTER 36

The weeks flew by, and Fife and Lily barely noticed the passage of time. They both worked during the week and had a standing dinner date with Annis and Joe on Friday night. Then, Saturday and Sunday, they went back into their honeymoon cocoon.

Jobs were done around the house later in the day as they rarely left the bed until noon. Saturdays were for tidying and laundry, and Sunday, they'd prepare a big dinner for just the two of them.

Suddenly, it was the day before they were to leave for the states. Fife had arranged to pick up Annis at the crack of 'bloody dawn' so that the three of them could be on the first boat to the mainland. Joe wasn't coming. The cows needed tending and the relationship needed time.

Lily asked Annis if she minded. "Joe not coming – no I don't. I realize that we sort of picked up where we left off when we were young, but we have still only been dating for 2 months in real-time. It will be good for us to miss each other." Annis said in a voice that brooked no further questions.

Their plane was leaving at two for Boston, and it was a long ride to the airport in Glasgow.

Lily had a feeling of excitement mixed with a whiff of foreboding. And she couldn't shake it. *'Surely, it's just because I've been away from the scene of that bloody awful day – that's probably what's worrying me,'* thought Lily trying to rationalize this unease she'd developed. But she was also experiencing a lurchy stomach, something she rarely did.

Once on the road, distracted by Annis' excited prattle, Lily felt better. By the time they boarded their flight to Boston, she was as good as new.

# CHAPTER 37

It was nearly nine pm when the Aer Lingus flight landed at Logan. Lily, Fife, and Annis wound their way through baggage claim with passengers from half a dozen other flights. Annis and Fife seemed to have new energy – excitement to see Boston and America for the first time. But Lily was dragging. She hadn't slept on the plane because of air sickness.

She'd taken Dramamine when they left, but it had worn off by the time they landed in Frankfurt for a layover. She was disgusted with herself, and Fife noticed that she seemed to be dragging around.

"Love, are you OK? Shall I take your carry-on? You look like misery." Fife said, biting his tongue at the last.

"I'm fine, Fife. Just not a good traveler," Lily managed to summon a smile. But inside, she was scolding herself. *So here I am, heading off to a family wedding – my wedding! And I'm miserable.* She shook herself – *Drop the drama, Lily. This is the most important weekend of your life. Forget your troubles; come on, get happy!*

And, minutes later, as she left the baggage carousel, she was – happy. For there, making all the noise Griffins were known for, was her family! Lily didn't realize until that moment how fortunate she was and how much she'd missed them.

Dropping her carry-on and leaving Fife and Annis, jaws agape, she ran to the closest Griffin she could – Pete. The big brother of all big brothers. He hugged her as strongly as she hugged him. And then the pile-on began. When she emerged from the group hug, she saw Fife and Annis smiling broadly.

"Griffins – please don't knock them over but meet my husband Fife and my mother-in-law, Annis! Lily announced and was nearly tackled by the rush of Griffins to the new family members.

Lily felt so much love and relief then. Everything would be OK. Home is where her family was. And now that family was in America and Scotland.

Ten minutes later, they were in a caravan of cars, heading to the hotel. Fife and Pete, already fast friends who surprisingly shared a love of the Stooges and various SNL sketches, were filling the quiet with a hurricane of conversation.

Lily relished the familiar voices around her. And she found herself surprised when Pete announced they were at the hotel.

Lulu and Colm were stopping at the hotel, and they'd have a drink together once Fife and Lily settled in their rooms. After that, Pete would take Annis to their parent's house, and the others would scatter to their own homes.

# CHAPTER 38

L isten Lily – here is your mail from your apartment – all seeming to be junk but it wasn't for me to toss it! You may want that J Jill catalog for all I know!" Lulu announced with some officiousness. Here are the keys to your rooms. I took the liberty of booking two since, it will preserve the mystery until your wedding on Saturday!"

"You are so bold – and remember, we're married so we've *solved* the mystery." Lily added dryly.

She was amused that her sister had booked separate hotel rooms for her and Fife. *What cheek! They were married, for heaven's sake! No matter - they were adjoining rooms, so no one would know where they slept. Except it was a shocking waste of money.*

Lulu and Colm would get the cocktails

sorted while Fife and Lily dropped their stuff in their rooms.

Pulling her attention away from the mail, she noticed that only one bag – hers was in this room. And the door to the adjoining bedroom was open. She looked in, and Fife was hanging his suit up and moving his clothing to the bureau.

"Don't tell me you don't want to sleep with me, Mr. McCormack. We're newlyweds, and what they don't know won't hurt them!"

"Ah yes, my bride. But I think it's a nice idea to spend the time apart before our wedding sequel. Tradition, my love, is important. So important that I'll ignore how much I want to sleep with you. But just for tonight and tomorrow night."

Chuckling under her breath, Lily returned to her room and picked up her purse to go downstairs.

Five minutes later, Lily and Fife joined Lulu and Colm at a table overlooking Boston Harbor.

It was cloudy and dark, the only visible stars, the lights on the many harbor boats. A lovely night to reconnect. And the foursome spent close to two hours laughing and chatting. His new family instantly accepted Fife, and that made Lily very happy.

In particular, Colm and Fife were developing a bromance. It wasn't surprising – both came from the same part of the world – Colm, an emigrant to the United States from Ireland 15 years ago, and now Fife – a Scot.

But the chatter between Fife and Colm gave Lily and Lulu a chance to catch up.

"Lily, I swear you look wonderful. At first, you looked a bit gray when you came off the plane, but that's passed, and I can see that you and Fife are meant for each other. I see how you look at him as he's telling a story, and your shoulders settle, your mouth forms a soft smile, your eyes twinkle, and your hand reaches for his. And he doesn't take his eyes off you for more than a second. I don't mind telling you how worried we all were before you went away. The bombing took the stuffing out of you, and we all feared you were lost in depression. But I think the trip to Skye saved you." Lulu took a breath.

"I was lost, Lulu. But in the back of my mind, there was Fife. I kept thinking to myself, if I just could see Fife, he'll set me right. And I had talked to him about it several times over the phone, but it wasn't enough. I wasn't with him for 30 minutes when I felt the tension release. He is such a good man. The love, really, of my life. And as for the grayness from the plane – that's another story. Walk me to my room, and I'll tell you. Fife and Colm won't miss us, and I need bed."

"Fife, my love. I'm going to bed in my individual room. Please don't fall into the harbor. I'll see you in the morning." Lily and Fife shared a long kiss, which surely would cause Fife to regret the single room he'd celebrated.

# CHAPTER 39

L ily popped into the gift shop and emerged with a brown paper bag on the way back to her room. Lulu knew what was coming but waited for Lily to confide when they were in the elevator.

"Lulu, I think I'm pregnant! Pregnant for my hometown wedding! Isn't that terrible?" She began to giggle quietly, and then her shoulders shook with laughter.

"Lily, that's wonderful! And it isn't like you're an unwed mother. You are married, and you'll be married *again* before this weekend is over. That said, I'm waiting for the test!" At the door to the room, Lulu took the key in a rush to get in.

"OK, Lily, get in the bathroom and get testing!"

A few minutes later, it was confirmed, and now Lily had a decision to make – tell Fife now or tell him after the wedding. Lulu encouraged her to tell him now – but Lily, a traditionalist, wanted to wait until her doctor confirmed it. But that could take time – they wouldn't be back on Skye until the end of the following week – and they were flying – *but I suppose since it's so early in the pregnancy, that wouldn't matter – I flew here pregnant!*

"Lulu, please don't mention this yet to ANYONE. I want Fife to find out from me, and I want to decide how to do it."

"Of course, Lily – I won't even tell Colm, but you should tell him now – imagine how excited he will be!"

"He'll be thrilled, for sure, but the pregnancy is so early; what if something happens?" I want to be sure.

"So, you think you're only a month pregnant? You didn't sleep with him when you went over there?" Lulu was teasing now – she knew how her sister was.

"No. We didn't. We hadn't seen each other in a year. We had to get to know each other again. We waited." Lily's sense of humor was absent. Lulu knew not to go any further.

"OK. Well, time to get your sleep. You're sleeping for two now. So, nighty-night; don't let the bedbugs bite!" Lulu moved to the door.

"You're happy about this – right?" Lulu asked.

"I'm thrilled, but just being careful. You see, Fife. He is a big happy puppy. I don't want him sad if this doesn't work out. It's so early." Lily reached out and hugged her sister.

"Thanks for your enthusiasm – It's nice to have someone to share with. See you tomorrow, Lulu."

# CHAPTER 40

Shutting the door behind Lulu, Lily leaned back against it and let the tears come. *Of course, I'm emotional – this year has been a rollercoaster*

.

Emerging from the bathroom 10 minutes later – in her customary camisole and pj shorts, she paused briefly and placed a hand on her belly. *What kind of mother would she be?*

Fife, of course, will be the dad involved in every sport and activity. He would joyously attend every PTA meeting and doctor's appointment.

*But how would she be, Lily wondered?*

Her recent experience with Andrew called into question her healing powers. And her stamina as a caregiver. She'd left Andrew when she had needed a break. But you couldn't do that with a child. You needed to be there every minute -- to assure their safety, mold their values.

*STOP, her inner voice told her – you will be a wonderful mother. You are compassionate, loving, and kind. Andrew's injuries were the result of madmen, and YOU saved many lives that day and after. You are saving your own life now. This is a new life – not only for you but the child you carry. This is your second chance.*

Lily knew all that to be true. And she'd wanted a baby all her life. But she'd given up on that dream a few years ago when she looked from the calendar to her empty ring finger. A missed opportunity…and she'd thought back to Fife. For years she had wanted a relationship with him, but it never felt like it could happen. He was in Scotland, and she was in Boston. And she was never in Skye long enough to take the relationship to that next stop. But now she was, and she had an epiphany: Her trip to Skye to recuperate was her body's way of healing and giving her that chance for a 'next step' with Fife. It was giving her the power to change her life and to change her future. All of which were fine and exciting. But what did that mean for Andrew?

Against her better judgment, she reached for her cell phone and made a call.

# CHAPTER 41

A ndrew was surprised to hear from Lily the night before. It was as if she read his mind.

He knew she was in town to be married: Andrew was fortunate to have been present when Angela – one of his nurses at the first hospital, had gotten word from Lily. She was to be married in the states on September 1st, and Angela was invited.

Andrew had become friends with Angela after he left his last rehab -- he needed to check in with a doctor when his wounds began to bleed. Angela remembered him, and they began dating. His relationship with Angela was developing into something more, and Andrew's attraction to Lily had started to wane.

He hadn't told Angela about his feelings for Lily -- She didn't know how close Andrew had grown to her. Andrew was glad he hadn't. The crush he'd developed on her was an outgrowth of his dependence on her in those early days of healing. But as time went by, his passion for Lily had changed to gratitude.

Angela filled a 'hole' for him. She didn't see his grievous wounds - he wasn't a patient. Andrew was a man. He was beginning to emerge from his anger, and his sense of humor had returned in some fashion. Angela's attention did what months of rehab couldn't - he began to feel like a man again.

Today he saw Lily as his nurse and indeed as his savior, but not as a life partner. And Andrew knew she didn't feel that way about him.

Now was a second chance for him in many ways. A new life with new challenges but also with someone by his side who saw him as he was now and not how he used to be.

So now, hearing from Lily, Andrew realized he was at a turning point. He could show her how much progress he'd made, and it would end their chapter.

# CHAPTER 42

Lily was now secretly happy that Fife had insisted (and stuck with) their separate rooms. She had heard him come home after one am. He opened the connecting door and sighed when he thought her to be asleep. Then, he closed the door, and she heard him getting ready for bed.

So now, Lily could escape early and deal with things. She tiptoed out of the room just after 6 am and made her way to the dining room. Asking for a table for two, she waited.

The call Lily had made the night before would ensure her closure with the past. A happy smile crossed her face as she laid her hand tenderly on her belly.

"Hi, Lily."

Lily started, even though she'd been

waiting for him. Regaining her composure, she looked up to see Andrew right in front of her, looking better than she could have expected and much better than the last time she saw him. He was still in a wheelchair, but she could see he had prosthetic legs, and he was looking confident and not sickly.

"Andrew, you look well, so well. I'm glad you agreed to meet me."

"I was grateful for the opportunity. I wanted you to know that your early help saved my life. I wouldn't be here today without you."

"I'm glad to hear you say that, Andrew. I felt like I'd abandoned you. But, for my own recovery, I knew I needed to leave." Lily found herself getting emotional and bit her lip to stop its' trembling.

"Andrew, seeing you has given me such a sense of relief. I wanted to see you to talk to you about my future. I'm married, you see, and I am having another wedding here this weekend for my family. None of that would have been possible if I didn't go to Skye and see Fife. I know that the horror of the bombings will never go away – especially for you, Andrew – and I feel them deeply as well. But I feel like I have been given a second chance to get my life in order."

"I am glad for you, Lily. I know you're

getting married. I'm dating your friend Angela, and she told me. I'm happy for you. As a matter of fact, I will see you at the wedding because I'm going as Angela's date –although, I won't be dancing. I was hoping I could take you with me for a little while this morning to show you something special." There was a tightening in Andrew's voice that, while barely perceptible, Lily noted.

"Gee, Andrew – I don't know. I'm meeting my family for breakfast at 9. Can we be there and back by then?" Lily felt the slightest tightening in her gut. What would Fife think? Should she tell him? Could she trust Andrew? Of course, I can, she reasoned.

And he had a driver with him. That, indeed, was another layer of protection. But Lily couldn't shake the feeling of uncertainty she had now. The Andrew she took care of in the hospital and the rehab was vulnerable, but she knew, ultimately, she could trust him. This Andrew seemed so confident and had an urgency she couldn't reconcile with their circumstances.

"I have a black car out front, and he'll take us right over. I'll have you back before 9. Please come."

"Ok, Andrew, if we can go now. And if you can, assure me that we'll be back before 9." Lily wondered if she should leave a message for Fife, but considering that he'd been up until after 1, she hesitated to bother him. It was only 6:30 am.

Andrew escorted Lily outside to where the black car was waiting. He spoke a few words to the driver as he was helped inside, Lily following -- still a bit nervous about leaving without telling Fife where she was going. And, because she didn't entirely trust Andrew, she turned on her phone and started an audio message to Fife.

Andrew, in the front seat, was unaware.

"Andrew, can you tell me where we're going?" Lily asked loud enough so that the audio on the phone would catch it.

"I want it to be a surprise to you. I feel like we both need a moment of healing." Andrew had no more to say on the subject.

The car was quiet, but Lily found herself with butterflies in her stomach. She looked out the window and thought she knew where they were going – but she didn't want to guess wrong.

When they pulled up outside the restaurant, she was sure.

"Andrew – this is where the bombing was, isn't it?" She asked as much for the recording as to show Andrew she was still engaged in the outing.

"Yes, Lily, I thought that this would be a good place to find the closure we both need," Andrew said.

The driver pulled the car to the side of the road – almost across the street from the Marathon Sports, where one of the bombs had exploded. The driver went around the car, got Andrew's wheelchair out of the trunk, and brought it around to Andrew's door. After he ensured that Andrew was seated and safe, he opened the back door and helped Lily out.

It was a beautiful September day, and Lily was momentarily comforted by the soft breeze. But then the realization of where they were and what had happened there overcame her. She hadn't been here during the bombing, and so she hadn't thought about how things looked at the site. She saw the carnage as it came into her ER but had deliberately refused to watch any news coverage. So, now in her mind's eye, she saw it. She saw the crowd's excitement as the runners came through to the finish line; she saw the families together and the couples, and then she saw and felt the bomb explode. She was screaming in her head and felt her balance go. *Is this how it was that day?*

"Lily, Lily! Are you ok?" Andrew's voice seemed to be coming from a distance. But it helped free her from the nightmare she was experiencing.

"Andrew! I never came here after the bombing, and now I realize how horrific it was. It was a miracle you survived it."

She turned to face Boylston Street – trying to shake the images that spun through her mind of Andrew and the Cullens lying, bleeding on the sidewalk. Lily remembered the little girl named Natalie who '*needed a lot of bandages*'; and the couple who'd just started dating months before the bombing and now were dead. Tears streamed down her face.

"Andrew, something good must come out of this terrible event! Some miracle." She turned back, and there it was – her miracle. Andrew standing and looking strong, confident and walking toward her.

"Lily, this is what I wanted to show you. There IS life after the horror. I can walk again. YOU have married the love of your life. For sure, it was a horrible test. For me, my life changed. But I'm going back to work. I can't be a patrolman, and it will be a while before I can work as a detective, but I'll work behind the scenes for the terrorist task force. Running through video feeds and researching suspected terrorists. I feel good about that. And on the personal side, I have found Angela. I think I have fallen in love with her. I will give it time because my emotions are heightened now. But I am ok. And you are ok.

"Andrew," Lily said, her heart settling down to a normal beat. "Thank you for bringing me here. I was caught up in my end of the horror. And it was cathartic for me to see where it all began. I now recognize that we have come full circle. While I am a bit wrung out from being here and imagining that day, it is an end for me. And a new start for my family. I am ok." And with that, she stopped the recording on her phone. She was no longer afraid of Andrew but grateful. For he had given her the closure she needed.

Less than 15 minutes later, Andrew dropped her off in front of the hotel.

"Lily, thank you for calling me. And I'm sorry for dragging you away. But I think you agree that it was a worthwhile outing. And you still have an hour before your family plans. So, now, be a bride this weekend. Have fun and give up your worries. I'll see you tomorrow."

Lily hugged him quickly and went back upstairs, wanting to get back before Fife noticed she was gone.

She was fortunate – he was still asleep. She debated about taking a shower or spooning her husband. Spooning won. And despite Fife wanting them to have separate beds, like a magnet, as soon as she lay down with him, his arm came alive and pulled her close. Bliss.

# CHAPTER 43

An hour later, she woke with a feeling of being watched. Fife, tousled and sleepy, leaned over her and said, "Mrs. McCormack, you are a naughty girl. Can't even wait for our wedding to sneak into bed with me. Shame, shame."

Lily heard the smile in his voice and, for the millionth time since she went to Skye this year, thanked God she had. This man made her heart stop and start. He was her rescuer, lover, and forever.

"Well, considering how late you were out last night, I expected you to sleep in, and I considered a quick cuddle a good way to wait for you."

"OK, well, we're late—no time for fooling around. The kids will be here to pick us up in 5 minutes --to the showers, ma'am!" "I'll just call them and tell them we need 15 minutes.

"Ooops! OK. See you soon," Lily leaped up and made for her room.

Ten minutes later, dressed in jeans and a gauzy sleeveless top, Lily adjusted her hair, pinched her cheeks for color (for the nausea had returned), and willed herself forward to the idea of breakfast. *Let it be a slow one,* she thought. *Fife is going to be concerned if I continue to look sick.* Lily knew how tuned into her being he was. Lily would ignore the queasiness to overcome it. The power it had over her was nothing compared to the power she had over it.

All her life, she had overlooked the drama and the negative by refusing to give in to it. Looking to the time, it would be over. The only time it hadn't worked for her was during the bombing. There was too much to overlook, too much to forget and move on from. But she was doing it now. Now, married to Fife and carrying his child, she was moving on, planning a future. A serene smile spread over her face.

"Mrs. Mc – ready to go? We're to meet the kids in the lobby in two minutes. You look wonderful.

It seems your outing with Andrew was good for you." Fife stroked her shoulders, happy to see her happy.

"How did you know? – oh, the recording! I must have sent it to you by accident. I'm sorry, Fife. I shouldn't have worried you." Lily said, now feeling she had overreacted by making the recording. Andrew had given her no reason not to trust him.

"Yes, it was lucky for me that I slept through it all. Seeing you back safe and sound was reassuring. But I wish that you had told me. I can see that you feel better, though, and I will find a way to thank Andrew for that. Please remember, though, Lily – I am your partner, and I will always have your back.

I would have come with you." Fife's tone did not give away the fear he had that Lily had put herself in danger.

"Fife, you're right. But I was only planning to have coffee with him. When he asked me to go 'someplace special' with him, I became concerned. That's why the recording. I found I had nothing to fear; Andrew restored me to myself."

"I can see that you're better. But listen, we must get downstairs. Later tonight, we'll go over all that happened." Fife felt relieved at the lightness he felt coming from Lily.

"Mmm, Breakfast! Can't wait!" Lily turned around and kissed Fife so hard and so thoroughly that he considered putting off breakfast.

"OK, let's go!" Fife directed Lily out of the room despite his desire to stay.

# CHAPTER 44

Forty-five minutes later, feeling better moment by moment, especially since she'd been able to hug her nieces and nephews and Fife's niece Melly, Lily scrunched into her seat at The Paramount on Beacon Hill, surrounded by chattering Griffins. Fife was enjoying it too – laughing as he tried to get a word in edgewise.

"Wait now! Which of you has the best story about Lily? That's what I want to know. And Melly needs to know as well. What is Lily's superpower? What is her weakness?"

"Lily's weakness is Chocolate and any romance!" Piped up Carrie – Lily's eldest niece.

"And her superpower is LOVE!" broke in Daphne – her middle niece.

"OK – I'm only hearing from the girls –

what do you boys have to say about Lily?" Fife prodded.

"Aunt Lily's superpower is that she will stand by you – no matter what," commented Jay

"– but she seriously knows nothing about cars, building – boy's stuff. Practical stuff," added Charlie – the youngest.

"Well, I know all of that – does anyone have anything embarrassing to add?" Fife added.

"Fife, stop! I'm as you see me." Lily chuckled.

"Well, there is one thing – she cries at anything sentimental, particularly when people sing in groups, especially patriotic songs. She's a sucker for those."

"Thanks, Aiden. Now, let's see what we can find out about Fife. Melly, dish!"

Melly, laughing self-consciously, "well, from what I understand from my father, Donal, Uncle Fife, loves a good romance too. He once found a regency romance under Fife's bed. But, more than that – he loves American football, tacos and can't watch any movies where animals are in danger."

Lily squeezed Fife's hand under the table.

This was the man she knew he was, but her heart reacted to Melly's on-target description. This man was forever.

"Oh, now! That romance wasn't mine – I borrowed it to kill a HUGE spider! I remember it!" Fife denied.

All in all, it was a fun, light-hearted breakfast, and Lily felt like a new person.

# CHAPTER 45

When Lily and Fife returned to the hotel, they cuddled together and rehashed the morning. Lily told him about the baby, never expecting the tears that rolled down his face.

They cuddled closer.

An hour later, Fife and Lily met their family for the boat trip around Boston Harbor. Although Lily had been initially excited for it, now, with her queasy stomach, she worried she'd be sick.

"My love – something for your purse" Fife handed Lily a brown paper bag. Inside was a package of saltines.

"Fife McCormack – you are my hero!" Lily exclaimed, a little tear forming at the corner of her eyes.

"I told you I'd have your back," Fife responded with a soft voice.

# CHAPTER 46

The rehearsal dinner that night was a true celebration. The cat was out of the bag about the baby. Fife was delirious with joy and told everyone about it.

Annis was happy to see Lily and Fife and doubly excited to have a grandchild on the way. Lily's parents were as well. A grandchild was a miracle to them.

The party went on until ten pm when Fife said his family needed to get back to the hotel and get some sleep.

That night, Lily and Fife shared a bed – Fife's superstitions having disappeared.

He turned to Lily, who lay beside him, and, laying his hand on her belly, declared, "Family meeting. Mom will always tell Dad when she is leaving to meet strange men. And Dad will be building young Master

McCormack his own room!"

Lily smiled and added, "I've learned my lesson, and let's wait to find out what the sex is, Mr. McCormack."

# CHAPTER 47

The wedding the next day could have been an anti-climax for Fife and Lily – they were already married – even had a baby on the way. But the shadow of what had happened months before gave a very grateful family much to celebrate.

As they danced their first dance, Lily whispered to Fife. "I feel new. I feel as if my life is truly starting today. And I am really looking forward to our lovely French honeymoon – pleasant surprise, by the way. So how did Florida become France?"

"My sister-in-law clued me in. It seems I must kiss you on the Seine, in the Louvre, from the top of the Eiffel Tower, and in the D'Orsay Museum." Fife said, raining kisses on her upturned face.

"Oui. Remind me to thank Genie!" Lily was grateful and anticipated each one.

\* \* \* \* \*

Lily's brother and Fife's new best friend, Pete, gave the best man's speech, and it brought the crowd to tears:

"First of all, it is my absolute joy to welcome Fife to our family! You fit in like fate would have dictated. You have made me believe that there truly is the right person for everyone. And you make us all believe in the healing power of love.

"I want to acknowledge one of our guests today – Andrew Donnelly. Andrew survived the terrible bombing in Boston last spring. My sister Lily was his nurse, as well as a nurse for many others. When she needed a break after that to restore herself, she went to Skye. -- that's where Fife was, and she knew he could help her heal.

Finally, after 'dating' for fifteen years, they knew the time was right to make it permanent. And now, the three of them have new lives because of love.

Andrew because of the love of his rescuers and doctors and nurses like Lily; Lily because of the strength and love of Fife; and Fife because waiting for her was the hardest thing he ever did, but he waited, and love paid off in the end. So, as my new brother-in-law told me last night – Love is the ultimate gift.

It heals, inspires, and catches on. Never regret loving."

# CHAPTER 48

Fife stood and drank in Paris before him. All of it – he now understood what inspired Lily's passion for it.

No matter where you looked, there was something beautiful – The Eiffel Tower, the Jean d'Arc statue outside their hotel – the Hotel Regina, the Louvre. And there were the Tuileries Gardens across the street where just last night he and Lily danced slowly to the filtered notes of *La Vie en Rose* as it drifted out of one of the boats on the Seine.

From his window now, he planned – he'd bring her here every year. He thought about how she lit up when she stood on the Pont des Arts and gazed at the Universite de Paris – the Sorbonne. Time was kind here. Lily renewed here.

But despite her passion for Paris, just this morning, Lily had rolled over in bed and said to Fife, "I want to go home. I want to go home and sleep in our very excellent hen house. I want to plan the baby's room. I want to start thinking of names. I want to start our life".

So, tomorrow morning after a final dinner tonight at another fantastic Parisian restaurant, they were going home.

# CHAPTER 49

Lily, my love, you aren't seriously going to work this morning, are you? It's Christmas Eve!"

Fife was annoyed. They'd planned the day together, and now she was working – after one call from the hospital. Naturally, she'd become a reliable fill-in nurse. Which was fine for now, but once the baby came, she'd be resigning.

"Fife – it's only a few hours. I'll be home by noon! And you're going with Annis and Joe to pick out a Christmas Tree -- I'm so glad they got together. Joe talked about her the very first day I met him at the hospital. I'm glad you brought her in to see him".

"Me too, love – I guess he was a favorite when they were in school, but then Dad came along...."

"I wish I'd met your dad. From the stories Annis has told me, he was a great guy. Shame he died as he did. Sudden death from a heart attack is so hard on a family, and you being just back from Afghanistan. It wasn't fair." Lily was grateful every day, but now that she lived with Fife, she could see his daily stress, and she worried about the long-term impact on his health. That's why she needed to get away today. Just a tiny errand that would take a few hours.

"Listen, my love; I will be home by noon—you'll probably be later because Joe will insist on buying you a pint, and you won't be able to resist. So, let's plan to meet at 2. Then we can finish decorating before our company comes. OK?"

"OK, but don't let them work you too hard. You are carrying the heir to McCormack Construction, after all. He is precious cargo."

"Understood." Lily chuckled slightly, knowing how excited Fife was about the baby, and though neither of them wanted to know the sex, Fife always assumed it was a boy.

The two parted ways with a lingering kiss, Fife getting into his truck and Lily into her car.

# CHAPTER 50

Lily was excited about her secret errand. Christmas was a time for surprises – that's how Lily always imagined it. And now she had one. But first, she had to get the ferry. She could have taken the bridge over, but she knew on the way back she'd have her attention distracted.

Danny Blair ran the private ferry with military precision. Every day, on time, despite whatever the weather presented. And he very nearly had a clean record. But there were the occasional storms that came up from the Atlantic, which delayed him. Nevertheless, today was a fine, clear day, and Lily anticipated a fine ride to and 'fro. She was meeting someone at the port, would collect her package, and be back on the return ferry.

"Danny, how long is your layover on the mainland? I want to make sure I'm on your return trip."

"Ach, I'll wait for you, lass. I know you're getting my friend Fife's gift – the least I can do is return his wee pregnant wife with his gift."

"Thank you, Danny. I told Fife that I was working a few hours – he'll worry if I'm longer."

On arrival, Danny helped Lily ashore and told her he'd be back in 15 minutes. *Well, that should be enough time*, Lily thought to herself. So, she sat on a small bench by the boat to wait for Jerry Cleary, who was to meet her.

Not more than a minute after she sat, she saw Jerry approach. Though she had never met Jerry, she knew it was him because he was leading Fife's Christmas present – a galloping Golden Retriever pup. The pup, who Lily knew was a female, was wearing a plaid pullover sweater which played off her fine white fur and made her look to Lily like a Gund stuffed animal. Ten weeks old and full of fun, Lily couldn't help but chuckle at the sight of Jerry (who was a mountain in plaid with a red beard) trying not to step on the pup as she wound around his legs.

"You must be Jerry! And this must be my Christmas package! My husband will be so surprised!"

"Aye, 'tis she. And I'll have you know she's the wildest in the bunch. We call her

Storm because she is one! I see that you have a little one on the way.

Sure, you want to handle both at the same time?"

"We'll be fine. Fife, my husband has a construction company, so after a time she'll probably go with him some days. She's lovely. I love an English Golden. Although, I grew up with a ginger Golden. I can't wait to take her home."

"She'll be a fine companion for you – a friend for life!" Jerry added.

"Thank you for meeting me, Jerry, but I see my ride coming back. Must get on the boat!" Lily shook his hand and took the lead from Jerry. As she approached the ferry, Danny returned.

"Ah! I see what Fife's getting for Christmas! Best ride inside, or you'll be fishing her out of the water!" Danny said with the wonder of a dog lover looking at a puppy."

"Yes, I agree, Danny. I don't feel up to a winter dunking to retrieve this imp!"

Danny handed the lead to Lily once she'd gotten aboard, and Lily went into the warmth of the cabin, which, God bless him, Danny had tricked out with twinkle lights and a small

Christmas Tree. Lily directed the very active pup to a spot by the window and tapped the seat beside her. Then, like she'd known what to do instinctually, Storm jumped up beside Lily and settled in with her head on Lily's lap. Lily reflected, a bit teary-eyed, that her most recent Golden, Ginger, had done the same thing. And she fell immediately in love with her.

Ten minutes in, though, Storm began to wriggle, and, thankfully, since there were no other passengers and the cabin door was closed, Lily let her down to play.

As they docked, Lily, who was all of a sudden tired; that's *what happens when you're five months pregnant*, she thought, wished she'd asked Annis along to help.

"OK, my love! Quick pee and then straight to the car!" And mercifully, she obeyed.

# CHAPTER 51

As she pulled into the drive of her cheery Christmas Hen House, Lily noted that Fife was not home yet, and she was relieved. It was chilly, and a wind was blowing, but she would light a fire in the winter lounge and pop on a little Netflix. The trip on the ferry had exhausted her more than she expected. Storm would make herself at home, and that's how Fife would find them.

An hour later, Fife arrived home to a smoking chimney, a mysterious bark, and the sight of Lily on the floor, an unfamiliar pup barking beside her.

# CHAPTER 52

Two hours later, Lily and Fife walked out of Portree General Hospital, much relieved.

As soon as he'd found Lily unconscious, Fife called the ambulance service. The pup was surprisingly quiet – as if aware of the seriousness of the situation.

Doctor Anderson - the doctor on duty, recognized Lily right away and soon diagnosed fainting spell as being caused by low blood pressure and advised a few days in bed. An ultrasound was done, and the baby was found to be healthy, which allowed Lily to breathe more normally. Fife held her hand throughout and promised not to leave her side until she felt better again. His silent prayers were answered when Dr. Anderson assured them that baby McCormack was thriving.

He didn't ask about the stout little pup who stood by Lily's size, barking for help, until they were in the car driving home. "Oh, my love! Her name is Storm, but you can call her whatever you like. She's your big present, and obviously, I was expecting to explain all that when you came home! And she took a shine to Ailie the kitten right away! Although, I'm not entirely sure Ailie feels the same.

"She's lovely, my darling, and extremely welcome. And, may I say, a bonnie Christmas gift. All I can add is I cannot wait until you see my gift. So, let's go home, lovey."

Annis and Joe were settled in on the couch when Fife and Lily came home. A dinner was bubbling on the stove; the lights were low, and a Christmas Tree stood in the winter lounge. Beneath the tree sat gifts of all shapes and sizes.

"So," Fife said, "Lily and the baby are fine. T'was just a bout of low blood pressure. Nothing a little relax won't cure."

"I was frightened for you, love. I'm glad all is well. We'll keep you quiet over the next few months," Annis said as she hugged Lily tight.

"Yes, and we have kept these two quiet – got them to respect each other," Joe commented.

"These two? What Storm and Ailie?" Lily said, craning her neck over the couch to see what Joe meant.

"Ah yes, lovey. I'm afraid we were thinking alike." Fife paused and leaned over the back of the couch and lifted out an identical English Golden pup. "This one is named Flora. She's one of Jerry Cleary's latest litter."

"Oh, my God! She's Storm's sister! I got her just now from Jerry's latest litter. Why wouldn't he have told me you got one too?" Lily giggled. "No wonder the two get along. They're siblings. Thank you, Fife. Thank you. She's perfect. Storm, honey. Come meet your daddy!

# CHAPTER 53

Later that night, tucked into bed and cuddling Ailie while Fife walked the Golden Girls, Lily paused to reflect on her great fortune of meeting and marrying Fife.

Her life had much more meaning now. She was going to be a mum; her husband supported her, cheered her, protected her, and lavished her with love.

They seldom argued. Here she sat in the perfect bedroom, overlooking the Loch in a room designed by Fife, clearly to share with her. She had not one but two lounges – one for the summer and one for the winter. She had a mother-in-law who she adored. Her husband was building another wing onto the hen house to provide two additional bedrooms for when Lily's family came to stay. The nursery was made in an alcove outside their bedroom. There was more than enough room for the baby, crib, rocking chair, and dressing table. A padded window seat featured a view of the mountains and was lined with books. This was a perfect warm place for midnight or middle-of-the-night feedings. *Sigh! I have unquestionably arrived at my bliss.*

She heard the door shut and Fife talking to his girls – Flora and Storm, about Santa and best behavior. Lily grinned and waited for Fife to join her. It was midnight, and it was Christmas Day.

"Lily, my sweet. Those two dogs are so funny. They curled up right away together in Flora's crate. We're going to need a bigger one as they grow." Fife slid into bed and pulled her close.

"A crate? No, love, once they have proven that they won't pee in the house, I don't want to crate them. So instead, we'll get two fluffy beds for them, and that will do. Unless you want to build them a room too?" Lily laughed.

# CHAPTER 54

The winter on the Loch was cool and stormy.

On a snowy, crisp Valentine's Day, Lily squeezed into the lovely faux fur coat Fife had given her for Christmas and joined Fife at church.

Their purpose was not only to Thank God for their good fortune but to add a new family member.

"Do you, Joseph Hamish Fitzgerald, take Annis Murron McCormack to your lawfully wedded wife?"

"Aye, most definitely, I do. But, Ach, haven't I waited fifty-five years for this day?"

"Annis Murron McCormack, do you take Joseph Hamish Fitzgerald to your lawfully wedded husband?"

"Aye, I do."

Starting out as a married couple in their late 70s/early 80s didn't sway Joe and Annis. They had waited for each other in their own way -- living life until the time was right.

And it seemed like every house in Portree was empty that day – everyone standing outside the church, clapping and throwing rice for Skye's most popular couple.

# CHAPTER 55

Lily had tapered off her hours at the hospital in mid-March. She was finding it hard to get around, and the hours on her feet at the hospital sent her home with swollen ankles.

By 7 pm, shortly after she settled down to read, Lily often could be found dozing on the couch. True to their nature, the pups were active, and Fife was their primary caregiver, but they could be found on the sofa at night, like bookends around Lily. Flora was the smaller one; she had a more docile temperament than Storm, who was known to hop and jump when dinner was served.

In contrast, Flora usually stood by quietly until her bowl was filled. Fortunately, Ailie, the kitten, now a lovely fluffy cat, ruled the roost, and the two dogs obeyed her. She slept at the top of the couch behind Lily.

"Fife, honey. I think it is because they're all girls, and the maternal instinct is kicking in. They recognize I'm having a baby, and they are keeping an eye on us. I think it's sweet. I'll make them move if you'll come over and give me a massage. My back is killing me."

Fife complied. He was starting to worry about Lily. She was looking very tired today. And he half considered calling in sick tomorrow.

"Lily, how about you and I stay in tomorrow? Rory can cover for me at the job site, and the two of us can lie in bed and have a lovely time. It may be the last moments of silence we'll have for decades."

"Fife, I love that idea, but I have a doctor's appointment tomorrow, and you have the electrical inspection on the Ferguson house. How about the day after tomorrow?"

"Yes, you're right. I know. But the doctor's appointment – I should go to that with you. What time is it?"

"11:30. That's fine. I'll meet you there."

# CHAPTER 56

Lily managed to get herself to the car, okay, but her back and ankles were killing her this morning, so sitting down in the car was like heaven. Taking a minute to relax before she set out, Lily mused about the day she would have.

The doctor's appointment was exciting and important. Surely, she would be having this baby soon. She had expected it last week, but nothing happened. Now it could be any day. Her sense of excitement about the baby being here was muted by fear – *what if I'm a terrible mother? What if my baby doesn't like me?* Smiling wryly, she admitted to herself that probably every expectant mom felt the same. Lily was no different. But today was different, and she should be on her way.

*I must be sitting funny in this car,* she thought.

*Why am I getting these twinges?* Driving along, every several minutes or so, she was getting a cramp. Then, ignoring what she knew those pains could be, she pulled up at the church.

*This is more important. God wouldn't send me into labor before I finished this errand. Surely.*

Gratefully, the door to the church was open, and daffodils danced in the breeze by the door. Beauty was out here. Life was going on. And for that reason, today, Lily had to pray.

Knowing that if she knelt at the altar, she would never get up again, she chose the front pew for her devotions. Today was a day she had feared for the past few weeks.

An anniversary. A solemn anniversary.

A year ago, standing in the emergency room of her Boston hospital, she didn't know that carnage was coming in the doors and that her life was changing.

She mourned and cried for the lives lost. For the lives like Andrew's and the Cullen brothers, for whom life would never be the same. Families had lost sons, daughters, and parents. They had seen the face of evil in the bombs that had blown up. And, despite the happy changes in her life, Lily was determined to do justice to their sacrifice.

One bomber had died and avoided justice. The other sat in a jail cell where he would be for potentially the next 60 or 70 years - until he died — a life sentence. But never enough for the lives, he'd taken and changed.

During her prayers in the church, Lily was aware that the cramps were continuing.

*I'm having this baby today, she acknowledged. That's a fitting tribute to those we've lost – new life coming.*

*RIGHT NOW!*

The cramps - okay, let's call them what they were - contractions were coming on top of each other, and Lily had to admit that she couldn't make it to the car, let alone the door. Smiling, for Fife always knew best, she pulled out the cell phone he had insisted she carry and called him….' no cell service. Are you kidding? God - help me here!

"Lily, is that you? Are you okay?"

Lily looked up gratefully to see Annis's Joe.

"Thank you! Joe, call an ambulance. I'm having this baby. Now! You need to get outside where there's cell service. Help!"

# CHAPTER 57

Two hours later, drenched in sweat, Lily welcomed Esme McCormack to the world. Her dad, Fife, always expecting that their baby would be a boy, had prepared a speech by which he would welcome young master McCormack and was momentarily dumbfounded as to what to say.

But being the man, she married – full of warmth, love, and humor and quick on his feet and thoroughly besotted with his new pink daughter, Fife began:

*Esme, welcome to the McCormack family; we're already grateful for you. You bring joy and hope. You are the culmination of a 15-year love story and the pot of gold at the end of our rainbow. You are fireworks and fairy bells. You are the answered prayers of your mother and mine.*

*Your mother is the first jewel in our family*

*crown, and you are the second. I have waited all these years for a child, and you are exactly what I have always hoped for. When he comes in a year or so, your brother, Finnigan Andrew, will be lucky to have such a brilliant and beautiful older sister. In the meantime, take every hug you're offered and give every Eskimo kiss you're asked for. Just remember, Daddy will give you anything you wish for and cherish every twinkle of your eyes.*

Fife finished – unable to go on for the lump in his throat.

"Fife, that was lovely. But did I hear you promise another baby – a boy named Finnigan Andrew – in a year?" Lily asked, equally overcome.

"I did. I had a conversation with God while you were in the ambulance, and I promised him that so long as you were well and the baby was healthy, I could wait a year or so for a boy – if it wasn't one -- and that we would name him after Andrew --a very brave man who recently had to start his life anew."

He leaned over and kissed his wife and daughter and then gently curled up beside Lily and Esme in the bed and held them tight.

"Life is good," Lily remarked.

THE END

# ABOUT THE AUTHOR

Meg McNamara - romance novelist and children's book author, lives on Cape Cod with her family, which includes a golden retriever named Lucy. Meg works for a cultural non-profit to pay the bills and uses her free time to write.

Her two earlier full-length romances are also written under the nom de plume CeCe deLuc and include "*Love Aix*" and "*I See France.*"

Meg has also written numerous short stories and a children's book set in Paris. The children's book; "*Little Noelle's Christmas Wish*" is set in Paris and imagines the Eiffel Tower as the World's Biggest Christmas Tree.